And Iris — oh Iris — began swaying to the music. She rotated her hips. The short skirt flirted with the black trim of her fishnets. Slowly, carefully, she slid each pearl button through the eyelets on her soft, pink sweater. I was seconds away from finding out about those nipples, those hard, red nipples.

The sweater opened. The red lace bra pushed her small breasts into high, voluptuous curves. The arc of her darkened areola teased against the bra. Iris danced without taking a step. Gyrating her full hips, she let her sweater drop to the floor. How delicate her body was. She was slender. She was small.

Unable to tear my eyes from the delectable plushness of her breasts, I lustfully strained to see a hint of her contracted nipple under the lace. Yes, oh yes — she pulled a strap from her shoulder. Yes. Yes. She pulled the other.

Marlee danced her way over to Iris. "So beautiful. So beautiful," she hissed. And she was right. Her strong hand grabbed around Iris's waist. As if depending only on Marlee's grip, Iris arched back, letting her hands fall to her sides. Marlee tugged the bra down and Iris's berry nipples came into view. A demanding ache in my cunt caused me to jerk in my chair. I wanted so much to push Marlee aside, to take Iris in my arms, to hold her while she leaned back. I'd press my hands up and down her distended nipples. I'd sway and twist and . . .

Personal Ads
by Robbi Sommers

THE NAIAD PRESS, INC.
1997

Printed in the United States of America on acid-free paper
First Edition
Second Printing January, 1997

Edited by Christine Cassidy
Cover design by Pat Tong and Bonnie Liss
    (Phoenix Graphics)
Typeset by Sandi Stancil

Library of Congress Cataloging-in-Publication Data

Sommers, Robbi, 1950–
    Personal ads / by Robbi Sommers.
        p.   cm.
    ISBN 1-56280-059-0
    1. Erotic stories, American.   2. Lesbians—Fiction.   I. Title.
PS3569.065335P4   1994
813'.54—dc20
                                                                    94-15978
                                                                    CIP

Dedicated to the Ruby slippers

Home is where you find it

Thank you for inspiration —
All the women that should have
could have
would have.
And my muse who knows...

Robbi Sommers

Writer of lesbian erotica, born in 1950,
part-time dental hygienist. Mother of
three sons. Enjoys attention. Appreci-
ates being spoiled. Intriguing. Complex.
Vivid imagination. Seeks interested
women who like to read. Inquire
within.

BOOKS BY ROBBI SOMMERS

Pleasures

Players

Kiss and Tell

Uncertain Companions

Behind Closed Doors

Personal Ads

Getting There

Between the Sheets (Audio Book)

CONTENTS

In The Blink Of An Eye....................... 1

Fiction To Reality............................ 4

Going Up 27

If The Spirit Moves You 46

Generous Reward............................. 69

Carnival Girl 89

Reflections.................................. 112

Rhinestone Pumps............................ 131

In The Blink Of An Eye....................... 151

IN THE BLINK OF AN EYE

Sunday morning, I lie in bed memorizing the pattern of shadows on the wall. She enters the bedroom and I search her face for some indication that she might reconsider. As soft as any kiss on my lips, one smile could change it all.

Sunlight spills through the uncurtained window and spotlights her in a silver haze. In that single, perfect moment, we linger between past and future. If I could corral this instant, net us in the frozen, solitary second before she speaks, I would.

"Here's the paper." Her words wilt like weary

autumn leaves stranded on the ground. I remember how, before, they'd swirl like bluebirds flirting with spring. Was there some way to bring the magic back?

Her blonde hair is tousled from sleep. Oversized flannel pajamas enhance her vulnerability. God, I hate that I hurt her. Hate that she stands before me like a wounded butterfly.

Her hand rests against the curve of her waist and her glance skims past mine. "I think you should look for a place today." Her tone is arid and I am struck with sudden thirst. As if we had never been lovers, as if I had never held her in my arms, I can no longer read her. A vast desert stretches between us. I consider falling to my knees and begging her to forgive me.

Beneath the green flannels, her plush breasts entrance. A rush of passion casts me into memories. When we make love, Pele churns fire. Thor flails thunderbolts. I remember how hard her nipples would get. Pink. Flushed with desire. Her body trembles in hard spasms and pleasure spills from her in tidal waves. When she climaxes, I'm carried by a sea of heated lava. Like this, she brings me to my knees.

Are her nights as sleepless as mine? Does she still imagine my touch in the empty darkness? To my knees I'd fall if she'd give me one more chance.

If I grab her, pull her to me, take her in my arms — would my love pierce through her defensive armor? If I kissed the breath from her and exchanged it with mine, would she remember how I filled her many times before?

She tosses the paper on the bed and turns away, disappearing from my room like an autumn evening. The classifieds top the stack. Several rentals are

2

circled. Wishing that change was as simple as an ink-bordered ad, I close my eyes.

I don't need her.

I don't need her.

I don't need her.

Why beg? Hell, I could have a new life in the blink of an eye. I grab the paper and zoom past the rentals to the personals. Certain there was a woman who'd be more than happy to spend time with me, certain there'd be a woman who wouldn't turn away, I scan the offers. I could have it all, and more, in the blink of an eye.

FICTION TO REALITY

Exciting erotic writer seeks intriguing woman to help bring her stories to life. Must be open-minded, creative and willing to take risks.
Dream up a plot. Set the scene.
I'll do the rest.

Just because I write erotica doesn't mean I have a jammed, packed-with-action life. The droll truth? My free time is spent at a computer screen creating vivid fantasies of the life I *wished* I lived, rather than life as it was. I've always wanted so much more. I've flirted, I've teased, I've worn desire like an enticing leather dress — all of this to tempt women to take a chance. I've had little success.

It's my characters that have kept my life tolerable. Bold, seductive — in back seats of cars, alleys, fancy restaurant rest rooms, they made their moves. *I want you, baby* — seated at a table for ten, an invented woman would sneak her hand up my skirt. *I need you, sugar* — in a subway station she'd unbutton my blouse. Imaginary women approached me, took me, had me. Passion seeped into kitchens and boardrooms. The neighbor's girlfriend watched me undress from a curtained window; the twenty-year-old computer tutor answered her door wearing nothing but an oversized shirt; the aerobics instructor called me in for an after-hours, special conference — and on and on. A frustrated sex writer, I lived in a dream world, always wishing for one of my characters to come to life and find me . . .

Short but to the point, the first note arrived by mail. *The butch of your dreams waits patiently.* Unsigned, with a postmark from Chicago, the sender's identity was a mystery. Didn't matter, the words — the intention itself — is what ignited the flurry of excitement. Somewhere in Chicago, a butch woman was thinking about me.

Needless to say, I was intrigued. The daily trip to the P.O. box transformed from a routine task to the focal point of my day. Would she write again? What would she say? Soon she'd reveal her name and address and then what? Future prospects suddenly widened.

Less than a week later, her second letter appeared. Not waiting for the privacy of my car, I ripped the envelope open right in the post office. The fast and fiery sentences seemed to heat the page.

I can make all your fantasies come true. Would you trust me? If I found you, came after you, would you let yourself go with a stranger? That is what you want, isn't it? I read your books, I know you. The butch of your dreams waits, patient.

If I found you . . . Although her seductive words glittered, a subtle darkness shadowed them. I reread the letter, uncertain whether I should feel alarmed or aroused. What if she was an obsessive fan? I pictured an altar, somewhere in a darkened Chicago bedroom. Covered with half-melted candles, plastered with photographs of me, the imaginary shrine would be the centerpiece of a small, otherwise undecorated room.

Could she *really* find me? The quiet worry nagged. A post office box number and an unlisted phone wouldn't get her very far. Great care had been taken to protect my privacy. But what if she could?

And if she could? Maybe, just maybe, she was simply a hot, interesting butch who knew what she wanted in life and went after it. *Simply?* Since when did *hot* and *interesting* fall into the *simply* category? Wasn't this what I had been praying for every night? The fantasy woman's letter was like sunlight burning through a wall-like fog. My apprehension withered in the heat. I folded the letter, tucked it in my bra and headed from the dingy post office to the seclusion of my home.

Would you let yourself go with a stranger? No question, I would. In a second, I would! Those suggestive words, those hot words, those insistent words kept my foot to the pedal the entire drive home. I knew the things, oh yes, I knew each and every delicious thing she would do. I hurried to my bedroom, tossed my jacket on the bed and the letter on the desk. My untiring computer was waiting for me.

I began typing, at first slowly, methodically. She would track me down. Perhaps at the gym? No ... that wasn't believable. At my office? How would she ever find me there? I closed my eyes to pull up a situation. Yes, there she was. At the post office. She'd be leaning against a Harley when I pulled in. Her short, spiked black hair and dark sunglasses emphasized her tough appearance. I noticed her out of the corner of my eye, but I don't realize who she is. It would have been a few weeks since the last letter, and I'd be anxious to get to my box to see if another had arrived ...

There's nothing but a Radio Shack flyer. Disappointed, I close the box.

"Looking for this?" I hear a cool voice from behind.

I turn. The woman from the parking lot stands behind me, an envelope in her hand.

Oh, she looks good. She looks so damn good. Tight black jeans. A white T-shirt. Her stance insinuates power. She has a strong chin and a cocky smile.

My fingers raced across the keyboard, hardly keeping up as the nonstop panorama unreeled in my mind. I could see her clearly in my mind and decided to delete the spiked hair, changing the look by adding a black and gold bandanna, tied low on her brow.

I reach for the envelope but she grabs my hand. Without a word, she escorts me from the post office, across the parking lot, to a side alley. She pushes me up against the building and presses into me. I moan. We both moan. I'm hungry for more, desperate for more. Her breath, hot on my neck, gives way to an uneven pant.

I pounded frantically on the keyboard, all the while feeling the rough brick against my back, the heat on my neck.

She rips open my shirt and the cold air stiffens my nipples. Any second someone could come around the corner. I don't care. I'm a risk-taker, a wild woman who has waited for this, hoped for this, thirsted for this, for far too long.

Her mouth is soft. Her kiss is hard. She forces her hand into my jeans. I spread my legs, let her in. I'm sopping wet. Sex juice soaks the crotch of my panties.

Images of her, of us, flashed like Midwest lightning. I stumbled from the computer, fell on the bed and pushed my fingers into my fleshy pussy. So wet, so incredibly wet — I whipped my fingers against the hardened, thick wedge.

"Yeah, baby. Fuck me good, baby," I muttered.

She doesn't stop, would never stop. On the edge of a good come, I squirm. I beg. Her rhythm is unbroken and she penetrates me over and over. Biting my neck, my breasts, my belly — she does not stop. My back aches. My heart pounds and she does not stop. In an alley, near the post office, somewhere in a dream, she does not stop.

* * * * *

The postcard, a black and white photograph of a curiously beautiful woman, arrived the next week. The model, wearing nothing but spiked high heels and a fedora, lounged casually in a luxurious sofa chair. Her long, slender legs dangled over the stuffed arm. Scribbled across the backside of the card was the simple sentence, *See you in April,* and nothing more.

See me in April? What did that mean? That she knew where I lived? That she somehow had found me? I sipped my tea and contemplated my agenda for the next few weeks. I had a book tour scheduled — Houston, Miami and New Orleans — then I was off to the March on Washington. Would she travel to a book signing? Did she really think she'd find me in D.C.? The options seemed farfetched. But what if she come, from Chicago, across the country, just for me?

I flipped the postcard back to the photo of the woman, took another sip of tea and smiled.

She didn't show — not in Houston, not in Miami and not in New Orleans. And when I hit the streets of D.C., among thousands of lesbians, I realized the unlikeliness of her finding me there.

But if she did —

In a small flat, outside D.C., I sat on the ninth-story balcony with my laptop. I closed my eyes, getting a feel for a situation. I could be in a bookstore and she'd be there. She'd recognize me and . . . No, I'd be at the rally and she'd be a parade marshal. Yes. She'd come to my contingent. Of course! She'd assume I'd be marching with my publishing company and look for me there.

She's wearing a baseball hat, turned backwards, and her flaxen hair barely touches her shoulders. Freckles are sprinkled on her peeling nose and across her tanned shoulders. Her Hawaiian shorts, rolled at the waist, are baggy and hang loose around her trim waist. The bright orange print is a pleasing contrast to the hot-pink parade marshal's vest that partially covers her black bikini top. She stops at my contingent and gives me a once-over.

"Gonna burn," she says, pointing at my nose. "Need sunscreen?"

"Excuse me?" *She catches me off-guard.*

"I've got lotion in my trailer. Your nose and shoulders —" *She presses a spot on my arm and the color blanches from light red to white and back again.* "Sun's hotter than it seems. Everyone's burning without realizing it." *She lowers her mirrored sunglasses and I'm taken by the icy blue of her eyes.*

"Thanks —"

With a tilt of her head, she gestures for me to follow. We work our way through the crowd, across the central grassy area and to a group of trailers parked off to the side.

"Redheads," *she says, shaking her head.* "Ten minutes in the sun and they're bright as tomatoes." *She unlocks the trailer and I follow her in.* "You don't get this kind of heat in California, do you."

"How'd you know I was from California?" *I ask, not really registering the implication of her words.*

She pulls a container of lotion from a shelf and

walks over to me. "Because I read your books. I know you." A shifty smile crosses her face.

Slowly, she begins to lower the straps and then peels my tank top down past my breasts. The lotion makes a slurping sound as it squirts into her palm. The thick, milky cream looks like a large scoop of vanilla yogurt.

"Turn around," she says. She spreads the cool lotion across my back, to my shoulders and my arms. "Did I mention how long I've been waiting for this?" she coos seductively. With firm, exact strokes, her fingers smooth the sunscreen toward my impatient nipples.

And then —

I gazed dreamily at the skyline of D.C. I visualized her fingers inadvertently caressing my nipples as she rubs the sunscreen across my chest. My nipples would contract to hard points and eagerly nuzzle through the thick lotion. *The dark red tips look like fat cherry chunks on a layer of fresh cream.* With little enthusiasm, I clicked the words into my laptop. The concept — too predictable? too trite? — fizzled.

A heated breeze shook the trees below into life. From the ninth floor, everything appeared distant, like pages from a mundane book. Warm waves of air scooped into my alcove. As if it rode the wind, I waited for a rush of inspiration.

Momentarily, the air settled. Should I have her fuck me in that trailer? Maybe we wouldn't go to her trailer at all. Another gust of wind washed over me and I sat motionless, still waiting.

Maybe we wouldn't even meet . . . maybe the

goddamned story bored me . . . maybe it was time one of my characters came up with an idea of her own. Frustrated and unwilling to concede, I shut down my computer and headed for the shower.

Festive parties and activities were happening all over Washington that evening. A six-page calendar listed the events for that night alone. Uncertain where I'd end up, I rode the Metro to Dupont Circle. I dropped by several events, but by ten that night I had settled in a dance hall packed with women. I was sipping a Dr. Pepper and checking out the crowd when out of nowhere a woman stepped in front of me.

"Michigan Music Festival, right?" She stood too close and I awkwardly struggled with a pressing urge to back up.

I shook my head politely and opted to perch myself on a nearby table. She sat down at my side.

"No, huh? I could have sworn —" Her coal-black hair fell across her brow and she casually brushed it away. Her eyes, so dark that it was impossible to distinguish the pupils in their inky depths, added a mysterious edge to her otherwise carefree demeanor. The woman looked intently at my face. "Hell, you *sure* look familiar."

Don't we all, I thought, bored by a conversation that lacked imagination.

"Wait a minute." She slipped from the table and moved in front of me. "Aren't you the writer of all those erotic stories?"

Before I had a chance to do more than nod, she

reached for my hand and gave me a firm handshake. "I recognize you from the picture on your books. Damn, I've read them all!"

"Yeah?" I shook hands with her, taking a second to consider her more seriously. After all, the conversation had taken an interesting turn.

"I was reading your last book and I thought to myself, I'd sure as hell like to meet this woman." She laughed, almost to herself, then gave me a wink.

"I suppose one should watch what they wish for, huh," I said offhandedly.

"Ab . . . so . . . lute . . . ly." Each syllable slid like a long, low whistle from her mouth. "And what does a woman like you wish for?" She peered straight into my eyes, then, as if distracted, turned toward the dance floor.

I had a thousand wishes but said nothing. She apparently wasn't that interested.

"I'm K.C.," she said quickly, her attention suddenly shifting back to me. Her dark bangs fell across her face. With a haphazard gesture, she flipped the rebel hair back. "Keep me company while I have a smoke?" She motioned to the door.

She strutted a few steps toward the exit then flashed me a mischievous smile. In a tomboyish way, her cuteness bordered on sexy. Her hair, clipped in a new wave, on-the-verge kind of style, was long on top, but shaved on the sides and back. I guessed her to be in her mid-twenties, yet she had an offbeat maturity.

With a commanding gesture for me to follow, her attitude pivoted from cute-boy to cocky. In a blink of an eye, this young-cat girl hinted that a possible panther lay in wait. A newfound interest for her

13

nudged me from the table, out the exit and to the lamppost where she lit her cigarette.

With a style peculiar to the butch characters that I created in my stories, she inhaled, blew the smoke from the side of her mouth, then squinted. Her cigarette never strayed from the tough, three-finger grip that my characters used. I was intrigued, teetering on the edge of a situation. Perhaps she'd take me to her hotel and seduce me with her charms. Or maybe we'd go for a late drink in some smoky cafe. After two shots of tequila, she'd fuck me in the restroom. The possibilities seemed endless.

She dropped the butt to the cement and smashed it with the toe of her black boot. "I'm staying in Virginia. Metro stops running soon." She glanced at her watch and motioned toward an oncoming taxi. The cab swerved to the curb.

One moment we were engaged in conversation, the next she was opening the car door. Although disappointment surged through me, K.C. was all smiles.

"You busy tomorrow at noon?" she said, as if it were an afterthought. Before I had a chance to say a word, she flashed me a saucy grin and added, "Let's get married." Her black-mirror eyes sparkled. "There's a mass ceremony in front of the National Archives. Meet me at —" She paused for less then a second. "— Eighth and Constitution at eleven forty-five." She started to climb in the cab, but suddenly turned, grabbed me and kissed me hard. "Wear something pretty."

She ducked into the cab and slammed the door. The taxi disappeared around the corner. I stared after her for a long, long time.

14

* * * * *

Even though the evening hadn't gone as I had hoped, an intense excitement rumbled inside me. It was almost as if I had stepped into the pages of my own book. An impromptu marriage to a stranger, just because she asked? And then what? A honeymoon, not to be forgotten! In bed that night, I recalled the almond shape of her carbon-colored eyes. I thought of her thick, plush lips, her high cheekbones, her distinct nose. I could imagine us in countless scenarios — cruising on a Harley, sailing a boat, speeding in a Porsche. She was that kind of woman, my kind of woman, the kind of woman that launched unlimited fantasies.

I reached for my laptop and brought it into bed. She would meet me at the ceremony, but we wouldn't get married . . . or would we? Didn't matter. We'd go from there to the restaurant of a fancy hotel and only order foods we could eat with our fingers.

I leaned back in the bed and closed my eyes. I could visualize clam broth dribbling down my chin and butter-drenched lobster smearing my hands. She would look at me with a hot sexuality. The very thought of her obsidian eyes — how they squinted with intention, how they suggested a dark sensuality — and the promises they held, had me spellbound. I remembered her thick fingers gripping the cigarette, her partially buttoned shirt revealing the curve of her breasts. Pictures of her — against the lamppost, hailing the cab, kissing me hard — raced through my mind like a fast-forward dream.

I dipped two fingers into my sex and thought only of her. As gooey as our butter-drenched feast, my slit was soaked. I swirled my fingers around the ribbed opening then scooped the moisture to my clit. It had swelled and felt like a flexible, round bead. I tugged hard on the mons, and my clit-tip jutted from the flesh. On each side of the tiny marble, up and down, light as a kitten's kiss, I sped my fingers. Fast flutters, that's how I like it. Fast flutters get me going.

Thinking of her, only of her, I jammed my fingers back to my opening and poked them in. One then two; two then three. I knew myself — I knew myself well. Up in the air went my legs. Back to my clit, my fingers swarmed. I twiddled and tickled, then rammed back to my slit. Three, then four fingers, legs spread and high. And if I reached back with my knees and forward with my hands, I could take my whole fist. Yeah, I do myself well.

She'd bite me and fuck me and fist me and have me. Out of my control, any way she'd like. I was a risk-taker, a wild woman. I knew the ropes.

Over and over I penetrated my expanded opening with my own fist. Fire burned the tight rim and sex cream spurted. Crazy, I know. Wild, I know. But good, good, good as it gets.

I was on the corner of Constitution and Eighth by eleven-thirty. Down the street, masses of people were already gathering for the wedding ceremony. In something pretty enough to please any butch, I waited. I looked up the street, then down, up the street, then down.

From a distance, I saw her. She wore jeans and a

dark suit jacket. Her hair had been slicked back, the same way the butches in my books styled their hair. Like she owned the street, like she owned the whole world, she walked with an attitude that made my knees go weak.

The rose she carried was long-stemmed and when she waved, it moved through the air like a small red banner. My stomach fluttered and my heart began to pound. An inexplicable impulse to disappear into the crowd, to hurry back to the flat, made me momentarily dizzy, but I held my ground and returned the wave.

She was closer. Once again, nervous tension tempted me to make a clean break. Since when could I do something as impetuous, as foolhardy as this? I barely knew the woman. And then what? Could I *really* go to a stranger's hotel room and have sex without a care? Maybe thirty, now twenty steps away, she quickened her approach.

"You look wonderful." She caught me in a hug, spun me in a small circle and then kissed me softly on the lips. That kiss was so sweet, so tender, that everything else seemed to dissolve. Suddenly, I was somersaulting in thick, spongy warmth. Over and over, around and around, I reeled.

"The butch of your dreams," she whispered, or was that gentle voice mine? I wasn't certain. Words were being whispered, secret thoughts spoken, as I turned in circles.

"C'mon, we don't want to miss the ceremony!" Without another word, she grabbed my hand and we hurried down the street.

The butch of my dreams. We squeezed through the people until we found room to stand. Packed together tightly, everyone was laughing, smiling, filled with joy. K.C. put her arm around me and pulled me close.

The butch of my dreams. Vows were uttered. A rainbow of balloons filled the sky. K.C. handed me a silver ring and kissed me again and again and again. Rice and confetti poured down on us. I had married a stranger. The plot suddenly took on a life of its own.

Like the butches I write about, K.C. was romantic. The ring she had bought from a street booth, just because "a bride should have a ring." And from every outdoor vendor we passed, she bought me flowers.

In front of the escalator that descended to the Metro station, a lone sidewalk musician played a love song. K.C. abruptly stopped, took me in her arms and slow-danced with me. We blocked the Down escalator until the song ended, but no one cared. It was the weekend of the march and Washington was packed with romantics.

I had a book-signing at a store in Dupont Circle from one to four-thirty. K.C. dropped me off and returned later for dinner at a cozy Italian restaurant. The day unraveled like a story. She was smooth, she was attentive, she was caring. She was all that a femme could have wished for.

Not once did she ask personal questions, nor did she reveal much about herself. At one point, when I did try to find out a little more about who she was, she put her finger to her lips and said, "Today, I'm the butch of your dreams. That's all that matters."

I'm a writer of fantasy, I understand certain dynamics, so I kept my inquiries to myself and let K.C. lead the way. Which she did, through dinner, through an evening walk through D.C. and finally to the lobby of the Hilton Hotel.

"You know," K.C. said as she escorted me into the vacant elevator. "I know you quite well." She pressed the Tower button and the door closed. "I wondered, if I ever found you, came after you, if you'd let yourself go with a stranger." She cornered me. "And it seems that you have, doesn't it?"

The unsigned letter from Chicago immediately flashed into my mind. "Are you Chicago?" was all I managed to say before she pushed her hand into my hair and covered my mouth with hers.

The door opened. "Tower," she said, her voice cocky. She escorted me out of the elevator toward a guard who sat at a desk at the far end of the hall. TOWER GUESTS ONLY, the sign above him warned.

As if preparing to question her, the guard evaluated K.C. She tossed him an of-course-I-belong-here look and walked past him. Trying to feign the same expression, I followed closely behind her into the private lounge.

"It's all a matter of illusion," she boasted, gesturing back toward the guard. "*You* know what I mean, being a writer and all." She snatched a couple of fancy hors d'oeuvres from a well-spread table and popped them into her mouth. "Can I pour you some champagne, Madam?"

"None for me." I shook my head and glanced back toward the door. We had cruised by the guard — no problem. Now that we had had that thrill, I was ready to move on, before we got caught.

"Let's look around." K.C.'s voice filled with a rebellious edge. "C'mon." She grabbed my hand and led me toward the rear of the lounge. We passed several couples who were seated on sofas. A few people watched the news on a corner television. The only one who seemed to pay any attention to us was a lone man. He sipped his drink but seemed to watch us intently.

Security? I wondered, nervously.

"Do you think that guy's watching us —" I started to ask.

"What's in here?" K.C. swung the door and clicked on the light. We were in the Tower Lounge bathroom. Thick, white Hilton towels hung from brass racks. Fancy soap balls filled a crystal dish on the sink. The toilet was decorated with oak and brass fixtures and a there was a curtainless tub behind the door. "Well-what-do-you-know." Her singsong words blended into one long phrase.

"Looks like a bathroom," I said and turned to go.

K.C. caught her finger in my back belt loop. "Whoa, not so fast." She pushed the door shut. "Let's take a bath." A wild streak flashed in her eyes and a clever smirk tilted her smile.

"A bath?" I gave a slight laugh. Oh, she was funny, wasn't she... *wasn't* she?

"Yeah, a bath." She started unbuttoning her shirt. "I'm an Aquarian. I need frequent dips in the water to keep me functioning."

"You're taking off your clothes, right here, just like that?"

"No, *we're* taking off our clothes. Think how refreshed you'll feel afterwards." She reached for the top button of my shirt.

"You *actually* expect me to undress?" I struggled not to sound startled.

"Sure. What's the matter? Is the hot, wild erotic writer just all talk?" K.C. looked me straight in the eye.

"Of course I'm not all talk!" I snapped. "You caught me off guard, that's all." I took a quick moment to concoct a good reason not to bathe. "It's my hair." I glanced in the mirror and thankfully gave my long hair a fluff. "It'll get wet. No hair tie, nothing —"

K.C. reached in the front pocket of her jeans, pulled out a thin brown hair tie and twirled it around her finger. "Just your luck," she said coolly.

I smiled a thin thanks and took the tie. Meanwhile, K.C. stripped out of her clothes and started the bath. The water made a thunderous sound. I figured that any minute someone — the man who watched us enter the bathroom? the patrons on the couch? the guard at the door? — would bang on the door and demand entry. *What's going on in there?* they'd all chime.

"You know," I said, trying to sound casual, "this is something my characters would do. I, on the other hand, am just the writer — we live different lives."

"And you think —" K.C. grinned. "— that it's *that* easy? You just write the stuff and then your characters are left on their own? I don't think so." Her words, *I don't think so,* had a singsong lilt.

She glanced in the mirror then turned toward me. "That kind of energy builds up, know what I mean? Builds and builds until your characters can't take it anymore. Tonight, with my help, your characters take revenge. We've come for you and are calling your bluff."

Naked, she stood before me. I tried to concentrate on the tattoo of a phoenix that rode her left shoulder, although my focus kept drifting to her plum-colored nipples.

21

"Well?" she said impatiently.

I deliberated the multitude of times that I had wished my characters, no, *willed* my characters to life. How could fantasies come true if I was afraid to step in when they appeared? I pulled back my hair, tied it with the elastic band and sat down on the toilet seat lid. It was best to begin by taking off my boots.

K.C. turned off the fast-flowing faucet and we climbed into the tub. She sat in the back and made room for me between her legs. I leaned into her, acutely aware of her erect nipples pressing against my back.

"I love water," K.C. whispered.

She dribbled water down my shoulders. The liquid streamed to my breasts, causing my flat nipples to stiffen to pink stubs.

"You like the water, too, don't you?" She lightly bit my shoulder, then trickled more.

"Yes." I closed my eyes.

"I thought so." I could hear desire in her voice. "I read your books. I know you." Slowly, yet firmly, she pinched my tender nipples, twisting and plucking until they stood from my breasts like dark red knots.

Again her teeth sank into my shoulder, only rougher, heavier, this time.

"I like your tits," she said in a low voice. "I like how your nipples stand out. How red they are. How pretty they are."

My nipples enlarged even more. A hot pleasure sizzled in my clitoris. I pressed my back against her plush breasts. "Yes, oh yes."

"C'mon then, baby," she coaxed. Her words steamed the room. "C'mon then, baby."

One hand still twisted my nipple. The other slid down my belly. Her fingers separated the folds of my pussy and slipped in. "You like that? You like that, honey?" she muttered.

I did. I liked that and wanted more. Much more. She eased her fingertip along my thickened clit and then around the lip of my opening. I tried to lift up. I tried to tempt her to plunge into my aching cunt. But she hesitated, merely tapping her finger on my vaginal slit and nothing more.

"Water's cooling." She moved her hand from my throbbing pussy and turned on the water. The pounding sound as the tub filled seemed to echo in the bathroom. I was more than certain the loungers just outside would begin banging on the door at any minute.

"K.C." I tried to keep my tone even. "It's warm enough, don't you think?" I felt suspended in that precarious moment between not-caught and caught. Visions of the headline, "Trespassing Naked Lesbians Caught In Act," stretched before me. I felt suddenly very undressed, very uncomfortable and very ready to get out.

"Warm enough? I don't think so," she replied in that same singsong voice she had used earlier. "Just relax, honey. And check this out —" Before I had a chance to argue, she lifted my legs to each side of the tub and slid me forward. The warm, nonstop flow of water splashed directly onto my clitoris. "Nice, huh."

"K.C. —" I tried to protest but the pressure of the water felt deliciously good. The headlines, the lounge, the image of the guard, all spun in a fast whirl down the drain.

"Yeah, that's more like it, isn't it?"

I had to agree, this *was* certainly more like it.

"Spread your legs farther, that's right, let me prop you up a bit. Yeah, how's that? How's that?"

Her persuasive words were swiftly sucked into the rumble of the rushing water and I had to concentrate to follow her requests. *Spread my legs farther. Lift higher.* And the relentless beat from the tap, the ongoing pouring from the tap, pressed and massaged my rock-hard clit.

She pulled my pussy apart with her hands. She bit my shoulder, harder and more. She whispered my name again and again. I arched and my clit was only inches from the spigot — and the water splashed down, the water smashed down, the water cascaded down on me.

She pinched my nipples, then stretched my cunt open. Pinched my nipples then stretched me again. As I jerked, I could see my clit, cherry-bright and swollen twice its normal size. She pulled me tight, exposing me fully. In nonstop waves, the water kneaded my clit.

She held me up, held me open. The water lapped like a giant untamed tongue, flattened me like a liquid rolling pin, massaged me like a relentless lover.

K.C. kept me right there until I thundered over the falls and into the abyss.

When we finally creaked open the bathroom door, the entire lounge was quiet. We were the only remaining Tower guests. K.C. grabbed a handful of nuts from the table and tossed them into her mouth as we passed the guard.

"You'll need more towels in the bath," she said matter-of-factly.

With a quizzical expression, he glanced up over his book.

"And washcloths." Laughing, she grabbed my hand and we hurried to the elevators. "Wasn't that great!"

I had to confess that it was. The whole scenario was right out of a book. "What next?" I asked, anticipating the rest of the night. We were back on the street. The warm night air felt good after our long bath.

K.C. squeezed my hand then signaled to an oncoming cab. "Metro stops running soon." She pointed to her watch. "Gotta run."

"But —" I tried to interrupt the sudden plot shift but K.C. kept talking as though she were in charge and I, an inconsequential character.

"To be the butch of your dreams, I *have* to leave. We both know that." She lit a cigarette, inhaling it with the style I knew so well. "After all, you know how these stories go."

The cab pulled to the curb.

"But that's not how *this* has to be..." I struggled to slow the story line, to get things under control.

K.C. tossed her cigarette to the street and climbed into the cab. "You're the writer. End it any way you like." The car door closed and she blew me a kiss. "See you in the pages."

The beat-up taxi pulled away from the curb and blended into the ongoing traffic. For the longest time, I stared after her, willing her to return, but she was gone.

Thinking of the situation, I hailed a cab.

From behind me, a car horn blares. I turn to see K.C.'s taxi swerve to the side of the street.

"I just couldn't leave," K.C. says, rushing to me.

Arm in arm, we head back to the Hilton and rent a penthouse suite. K.C. requests champagne, fruit and extra towels be sent up to us. Room service is delivered by a very attractive butch woman. The cut of her slacks and shirt emphasizes her strong, stocky build. She looks at us. We look at her...

GOING UP

Intense, passionate Scorpio seeks sytraitlaced businesswoman interested in shedding her inhibitions. You're very feminine in your tailored suit, stockings and heels. You work in the financial district and spend most of your time riding elevators from one meeting to the next. Looking for more? Tell me the building, the elevator and the time you'll be there. I promise a conference you'll never forget.

The general complaint from Sylvia was that I was a workaholic. It's not true. Dedicated to my career? Yes. Take an active role in being successful? Yes. But married to the job? I think not.

Unfortunately, Sylvia refused to release me from her continual you-work-too-much grievance. She'd stomp around the flat, grumbling that if it wasn't for sex, I'd never come home. "Too bad you can't just grab someone in an elevator and do it there," she'd gripe. "You could save yourself the fare home."

At first, I'd fall into her little scene. "You like where we live, don't you?" I'd snap back. "You like the expensive clothes that my salary allows you to buy, don't you?"

Sylvia would stand there with a glare in her eyes, but she'd always start to waver when faced with that sort of foolproof argument. After all, she did like the clothes. We both knew that.

Her mouth held a seductive pout when she was angry and her full lips, red with creamy lipstick, would resemble her scarlet pussy. The similarity always gave me a motivational shove toward fast negotiations.

"Baby, I'm sorry that you're mad," I'd concede.

"I just miss you," she'd whimper. Her mouth would fall into that sugar-sweet sulk and I'd have no choice but to grab her and suck her luscious lips into my mouth. On the floor, the couch, the table — wherever we were — we'd temporarily settle our differences. Sylvia liked being fucked this way. I liked doing it and it all seemed to work out just fine . . . until out of the blue, Sylvia left me.

The bad news came in a six-page, you're-a-workaholic letter. Her last caustic words, *try the elevators,* blazed from her expensive lilac stationery. There was no room for negotiation this time, no way to sway her with my Scorpio charm. She refused my calls and returned my letters.

28

Not until Sylvia was gone did I realize how much she had brightened my otherwise drab apartment. I fell into an acute depression. My incentive to leave the office lessened and I began staying later, only going home to sleep. Once or twice, I didn't even make it back to the flat and woke up early in the morning, sprawled across my office couch.

As the weeks passed, I realized that it wasn't actually Sylvia I missed — it was the fast and volatile sex. I recalled the good old days when I'd work late and Sylvia would get angry. God, her indignation aroused me. In her sexy, pouty way she'd leave me no choice but to take her.

There were so many scenarios. One time I had come home, even later than usual, with a large peace offering of daisies in my hand. Fortunately, I'm fast on my feet and dodged the small pillow she hurled across the room at me.

"Where have you been? Why didn't you call?" Her cheeks were flushed and her eyes flared.

"I got held up in a last-minute meeting." I offered her the bouquet.

She grabbed the flowers and flung them around the room. "I could give a shit. You never think of me. You could have at least called." She tromped to the corner of the living room and crossed her arms.

"I didn't call —" I retrieved one daisy from the floor. "— because I was busy making —" I picked up another. "— big bucks for a pretty new dress —" I slowly moved toward her, gathering the daisies. Her breath quickened. She knew what was coming. We both knew what was coming. I reached her, pushed my hand into her long, strawberry-blond hair and tugged. "— for my sexy, sexy baby."

29

The mention of a new dress, waiting right at that moment in some nameless store, caused Sylvia's coral-colored sulky mouth to edge into a restrained smile.

"I hate when you're late." She sighed.

"And I hate when you're angry," I whispered, handing her the daisies. "Hate it. Hate it. Hate it." I clenched her silky hair between my fingers.

Her exotic fragrance was unfamiliar. Had she shopped for an addition to her French perfumes? The idea excited me. The scent excited me. Without caring, I tightened my grip on her hair. She moaned in pleasure. I knew her. By now, her nipples would be hard, her pussy would be wet.

"God, you smell good. Is that a new perfume?"

Her ruby lips were so plush, so ripe. It took everything I had to stay in control.

She nodded slightly.

"A woman like you should have everything she wants."

Sylvia dropped the bouquet to the floor. Her eyes were closed. Her thick, succulent lips were slightly parted. Desire permeated the room like a steaming vapor. With each breath, I craved her more.

"What do you want now?" I spoke in a deep, provocative tone. "What does my Sylvia want right this minute?"

"You," she muttered. "I want you."

"And do you know what *I* want?" I guided her toward the glass dining table. "And how I want it?"

Sylvia glanced at the table and then at me. "Oh yes," she said, sliding up on the table. "I know exactly what you want."

One thing about Sylvia — she knew how to please. When I returned from clicking on the stereo, she was already on the glass table in a squatting position, her skirt hiked to her thighs.

I crawled under the table and looked up at the glorious sight. My Sylvia, directly above me was pantyless. She spread her legs slightly and the large, bulky lips of her pussy fell open. Her deep pink clitoris hung like a juicy sliver of watermelon. Sex dew lined the reddened rim of her slightly opened slit.

It made me crazy to have the partition of glass between us. I loved it — hated it. I ran my fingertip along the smooth glass. She lowered herself, dropping her meaty clit closer. I imagined sliding my finger into her slick, warm crease and dragging the moisture from the well of her vagina to the bulky, rose-colored clit.

Sylvia pulled her lips open and flicked her pulpy clit with her finger. Automatically, the flesh compressed, causing the pebble-like clit-tip to poke out. Back and forth, she wiggled the pleated skin, occasionally lingering on the knotted pearl and then slipping down to the now gaping, oily slit.

Sylvia. Sylvia. Sylvia. Just the thought of her pussy smeared on the glass made me wish she'd be waiting for me when I got home. But she wouldn't be. Those days were over. Instead, I'd sit at my desk, well past six, thinking about the way it used to be.

I was a passionate woman with a high sex drive. I knew what I needed, but with my schedule, taking time and energy to meet, date and finally have sex — without all the messy complications — seemed overwhelming. How and where I'd find release was fast becoming a major concern.

It was one of those work-late-no-hurry-to-get-home nights when the brilliant idea struck. I was riding from the nineteenth floor to the lobby when the elevator stopped on ten. A woman stepped in. She offered me a timid smile and glanced at the lit Lobby button.

"Lobby?" I asked.

Stiffly restrained, she nodded then glanced at the row of numbers above the elevator door.

"Lobby it is." For no reason, I pushed the Lobby button again. She focused on the line of numbers. I focused on her. My shirt was wrinkled from sitting too long. With every decision I had made during the course of the day, my hand had pushed through my bangs — leaving my hair a disheveled mess. Compared to her, I was in total disarray. Even after-hours, her conservative, down-to-business look was rigidly intact. Her suit appeared freshly pressed, as if she had dressed only minutes before. She projected a straitlaced demeanor but the narrow cut of her skirt did little to distract from the sensual curve of her hips and ass. The black suit jacket was securely buttoned, but I suspected her breasts were just as voluptuous.

Her raven hair, pulled into a tight French twist, suggested a cool severity although rebel wisps had escaped the hairpins' wrath to frame her face in sexy softness. In a quick glimpse, I imagined pressing her against the elevator wall. I'd let down her hair and revel in its perfumed sweetness. Fierce kisses — on her cheeks, her neck, her shoulders. In an instant, her prim business shirt would be unbuttoned. In an instant, I'd suck her hardened nipples into my mouth.

I cleared my throat and she glanced at me. Beneath a white lace bra, her full breasts waited to be caressed. She'd murmur no, but mean yes. I'm a Scorpio. I understand these things. She'd unzip her skirt for me. She'd pull her panties down for me —

The image of her half-dressed and hot with desire rode my shoulder like a bantam demon. It coaxed me with nonstop whispers. *C'mon, take her. C'mon, grab her. Say something before it's too late. She's yours for the asking. It's written all over her prissy face.*

"Didn't think many people stayed here as late as me," I said as casually as possible. The imp hissed in my ear. The bell clinked and the elevator door slid open.

"Guess not." She headed toward the entry. I quickened my pace to keep up with her.

"They say I'm a workaholic," I offered, as if this confession would bring us to a common ground. "I'm here late most of the time."

"Not me," she replied.

She moved swiftly past the night guard, who unlocked the door for us. As if cued, a long black Mercedes pulled up. The car door swung open before I had a chance to get any further.

"Don't work too hard," she said over her shoulder as she climbed into the sedan. Some man, some good-for-nothing man, was behind the wheel.

"Hi, baby," he muttered.

Kick the car, the invisible rogue on my shoulder insisted.

She gave him a kiss on the cheek.

Kick the damn car.

Without another word, she closed the door and they drove off.

G-o-o-d job. The sharpness of the whisper bit my ear.

The vision of her large, erect nipples consumed me. I stuffed my hands into my coat pockets and kicked a bottle cap across the sidewalk. What if I had made a play for her in the elevator and she had liked it? I'd have pushed Thirty-six and we'd have gone up to the top floor and back down again, maybe once, maybe twice — but not *too* many times — her Mercedes would be waiting and she'd have to run.

I kicked the bottle cap again, then again. The repercussions of a pointed, harsh rejection had cramped my Scorpio style. What if I had known for certain that she had wanted it? What if we met solely for the purpose of elevator sex? Fantasies started tumbling, one after the other, springing my ingenious plan to life. Back to my office building, to the elevator — *she'd be conservative and inhibited, but waiting to be undone, and God, how I was going to love undoing her* — to the nineteenth floor and finally to my desk, I hurried.

Intense, passionate Scorpio seeks... Without much thought, I typed. *You work in the financial district.. . riding elevators... looking for more...*

Either my muse or my sex drive had taken over. The words flowed naturally. I thought of the woman in the elevator and smiled. Within five minutes, the personal ad was in the building's mail slot. With a whistle and a wave, I bid the near-dozing guard good-night and headed home.

* * * * *

Placing the ad gave me impetus to leave at lunch and head for my P.O. box. Empty-handed, I'd return to the office and alternate between my work and my fantasies. I didn't expect a tremendous response. After all, how many straitlaced women wanted to be fucked by a stranger in an elevator? But I *could* imagine someone like Sylvia, dressed for a day's work as a temp, meeting me. Sylvia knew how to play a scene. She'd dress conservatively, but underneath her standoffish attitude and her businesslike demeanor, there'd be a firestorm waiting to be sparked.

I could envision her in the elevator. Her hair pulled back in some sort of twist; she'd be staring at the overhead floor numbers, just like the raven-haired woman had done. Thick-framed glasses would add to her prim and proper style. Perhaps a pen would drop to the floor and when she stooped to retrieve it, I'd have no choice but to notice the black trim of her stocking and the garter belt strap.

I fell into my fantasy. I was pushing the elevator button for the thirty-sixth floor. I'd take her up, all right. I'd take her up so high she'd never come down. She was detached and aloof but what she wanted was written all over her pretty face.

As the elevator cruised up, I played it smooth. I decided not to take her in the elevator, to make her wait. The door opened at thirty-six. Neither of us moved. The door shut.

"Going down?" I kept my voice steady, but my entire body buzzed with excitement.

Sylvia-the-temp batted her eyes and smiled. "I'm

35

so lost. I can't remember what floor my interview is on."

The sex energy seeping from her compelled me to step closer. I cornered her, my lips millimeters from hers. "You could come to my office and call them from there."

"Oh, that's so sweet," she cooed.

Without looking, I pushed all the buttons. I kissed her again and again. The car headed down, the doors opened and closed. Down again, open and close. I unbuttoned her blouse and lowered the silk bra cup from her small breast. Her nipple hardened with the slightest flick of my tongue. Under her skirt, the sheer stocking reached just to the softness of her thigh. I slid my hand across the nylon to her warm flesh and uncontrolled excitement burst from my belly to my chest to my arm. Stirred by the intensity of the blast, my hand whizzed to her pussy. Three fingers plunged in.

"And the phone is where?" Sylvia pulled away and adjusted her skirt.

"N-nineteen," I stuttered, forcing myself to get a grip on the situation. Sylvia liked to tease and so did I. Using everything I had, I backed off. My fingers were pussy-wet and sticky. I gritted my teeth and pushed button nineteen again.

Twenty-one. Twenty. Nineteen. I led her to my office. Once inside, I locked the door. Sylvia went directly to the phone. She sat in my large desk chair and crossed her legs provocatively. The revealed black lace of her hose, the whiteness of her thigh, tempted me to come get her.

I was at her feet in seconds. She spread her legs

over the chair arms and her uncovered charms were in full view. Her musky scent surrounded me. Her large pussy lips fanned apart. Like a pink, ruffled ribbon, her showy clit perched right in the center of the strawberry-blond backdrop.

I flipped my notes over as if I'd find some trace of Sylvia's sex dew smeared on the desk. Sylvia. Sylvia. Sylvia. I doodled her name in black and filled the balloon-shaped letters in with a red marking pen. If I had her in this office? If I had her, legs spread and ready, in this office, on this desk?

I considered the red marker — its stubby flat tip, its cherry-red hue. Non-toxic, it said. Easy to use, it said. I streaked a thick, red line on my palm. What if she were with me now? What if she was on my desk — legs apart, panties ripped aside — right this very minute?

I closed my eyes and brought her to me . . .

. . . she was on the desk. I grabbed the red marking pen and tickled her clitoris with the wide felt tip. At first, the sex flesh seemed to suck up the red tint but I keep rubbing until the wrinkled skin took on the bright red hue. The sight of her pussy, extended and stained, threw me into a hard sex-ache. I doodled her cunt and tightened my own pussy simultaneously. The sensation of building pleasure made the room appear to vibrate.

I traded the red marker for hot pink. This time, I

stretched back her mons and exposed the rounded pink clit hub. With exacting care, I colored it with the pink.

Sylvia jerked, grabbed my hair and tugged hard. Her pussy broke into a slow grind. I could read her — she was ready to be penetrated. I flipped the marker and inserted the other end into the oily opening. The slight clicking noise made me so hot I could hardly keep a steady, slow rhythm going. But I concentrated, fucking her nice and easy with the marker. The end went in and out, in and out, each stroke layering a treasure of slippery silk-come on the pen. I got crazier, hungrier, for her.

Her fat clit dangled from her pussy like a chunk of pomegranate pulp. A sudden thirst parched my throat and I smeared a finger full of her sex juice across my mouth. She tasted tart, as if she'd been waiting weeks to be fucked. I plunged my tongue into her creamy slit and lapped in fast circles, over and over. Eyes closed, I still saw the image of her crimson cunt. Her pussy would cover my face with wet folds and soft hair. And somewhere in the dampness, I'd lose myself for hours.

The fantasy of Sylvia and me, right here in my office, was so vivid that I had to take a moment to bring myself back to reality. Unmercifully aroused, I had no choice but to advise my secretary that I wasn't to be disturbed, to lock my office door, and to unzip my pants.

It was crazy, I know, but I couldn't stop myself. Pants off, I straddled the desk chair, just like the image of Sylvia had. What harm if I just uncapped the red marker and used it on myself. Non-toxic, right? It hadn't hurt my palm, had it? On a lark, I spread my pussy lips and trailed a thin, scarlet line across my clitoris. The pen tip was a flat, rectangular shape. The texture was rigid, like a cool, hard sponge. I streaked it down my clit-ridge — each colored stripe made me harder.

It felt good, so good that I didn't stop. I grabbed a yellow marker and pushed it into my cunt, all the while painting my clit brick-red. I dipped the yellow marker faster, scribbled the red. Sunk the yellow, whipped the red. Flashes of Sylvia squatting on a glass table, opening her pussy wide, and of the raven-haired businesswoman letting me fuck her in the elevator, consumed me. The slapping sound of the marker as it drove in and out made me wild. My clit was blood-red. Again and again, I rammed the marker, stabbed the marker, lunged the marker until, in a silent flurry of sparks, I came at my desk.

All I needed was one single reply. Somewhere in this city, there had to be a woman who was looking for more. Each day, I'd leave the post office empty-handed but excited. I had a sense she was out there, getting ready to make her move.

When the reply finally arrived, I was ecstatic. Her elegant handwriting looped in smooth curves across the expensive stationery. Her words were short and to the point. *Yes, I work too much. Yes, I'm looking for more. Tell me where, when. I'll be there.* There was no name, just a phone number.

I called her immediately.

"Where and when?" The curt voice of her answering machine caught me up short.

I left my office address along with explicit directions. "I'll tell the guard to expect you. Be on the far right elevator and keep riding until I get on. This Thursday. Eight p.m. I can't wait."

The week breezed by and life felt great. By the time Thursday arrived, I was raring to go. At six, I rode to the lobby and let the guard know a business associate would be meeting me at eight.

"Working late again, Ms. Thompson?" He had a sympathetic smile.

"Well, somebody's got to keep that company running." I gave him a mock salute and rode to nineteen. Two hours to kill.

At seven-fifty, I headed for the elevator. I waited in the foyer, alert for the sound of the elevator's ascent. Nothing. I paced, then leaned against the wall, paced some more then leaned against the other wall. By eight-oh-five, I was steamrolled by tension. I pressed the button. The car reached nineteen, the door pulled open and I got in. Empty. Didn't matter, I'd wait until she brought me to her.

The door closed and the elevator remained motionless. Any minute she'd cross the lobby, press the button and I'd start down. In the corner mirror, my distorted image appeared curved and far away. I stepped closer, appraising my reflection — my shirt wasn't wrinkled, my hair was okay. Wanting to look good for my rendezvous, I had hardly moved all day.

The elevator jolted into a descent. My heart started pounding. I moved from wall to wall, trying to ascertain my best stance. She was seconds away. I could sense her, wet with desire, waiting for me in the lobby.

I froze when the elevator stopped at ten. The door slid open and in stepped the raven-haired woman. Hadn't she said she didn't work late very often? Why the hell was she here tonight? The last thing I needed was a third party along for the ride.

She gave me a peculiar look, then glanced at the unlit buttons. "Going down?"

I pressed Lobby. I wanted her out of my elevator as soon as possible.

"Working late again, huh?" She glanced at me then focused on the lit numbers.

I nodded and pressed Lobby again. *Out. Now.*

The car stopped at the ground floor but as the door opened the woman abruptly pressed Ten again. "I've left my coat. I've got to go back." She seemed suddenly nervous. She blocked the closing doors with her arm, waiting for me to exit.

No way was I giving up the elevator. In a tawdry display of poor dramatics, I hit my forehead with my hand. "And *I've* left my keys."

She glared at me. I glared at her. This was my elevator. Period. I pressed Nineteen. So there.

Up we went. At ten, she got out. I went to nineteen. I debated pressing the Hold button for five minutes to keep her out of my car, but I worried that my date would soon arrive. The car stood a few more minutes then began a descent, plunging me into a gnawing anxiousness. What if the woman got back on? What if my date had arrived?

The car stopped at ten. When the door opened, the woman stepped in. "Find your keys?"

Did I detect a snooty sarcasm? I pulled my keys

from my pocket, jingled them and shot her a phony smile. *Of course I found my keys. What did you think, that I was just riding the elevator?*

It was then that I realized she didn't have her coat. She spoke before I had a chance. "I've misplaced my coat." She shrugged nervously, hardly looking at me, yet I felt an intense energy building in the car.

She fidgeted with the clasp on her purse. The elevator seemed to reverberate with tension. Unmistakably uneasy, almost as if she had been caught with her hands in the till, she stared at the floor.

I wondered what she was up to, riding up and down in my elevator, after eight on Thursday night. I stared at her intently. Slowly, her focus moved from the floor to my face. It was in that single moment when her eyes met mine that I realized exactly what was what.

"You're looking for more than a coat, aren't you?" I risked.

She nodded then glanced back to the floor.

A rush of excitement plowed through me. Who would have guessed, in this whole city, that she would be the one to answer my ad. Things that are meant to happen, one way or the other. And now, my straitlaced, looking-for-more beauty was waiting for me to make my move.

"And you've been waiting for me, haven't you?" I stepped closer.

Still looking down, she nodded again.

"When I saw you that first time, I was so attracted to you. That's the reason for all of this," I said softly, trailing my finger along her cheek. She seemed fragile and shy. Was I her first woman? I suddenly regretted that we were in an elevator. She had taken a big step and deserved so much more.

With a look that could first melt, then boil any possible inkling of fragility, she stared straight at me. "I only want this to happen once." Her tone scorched. Passion blazed in her eyes. "Fast." She began to unbutton her silk shirt.

Momentarily taken aback, I was quick to regain my composure. *Once and fast.* I pushed Thirty-six and the elevator started to climb.

She pulled open her blouse. Her dark areolas seemed overstated behind the sheer white cups that stretched tight across her ample breasts. The confining bra was incapable of flattening the desperately hard nipples that projected out like square rocks.

I ran my finger across the cleavage of her breasts. She was feather-soft and perfumed. All I could think of was unhooking her bra — unsnapping that thin, transparent material — and burying my face in her cream-colored flesh. Once and fast.

I jerked down her bra cup. Her wide areola folded into itself, becoming a dark, wrinkled pedestal for the overextended nipple. A pinch, a twist — her nipple was rigid between my fingers. A pinch, another twist, and she began to grind her body against mine.

I pulled up her fancy business skirt and yanked aside flimsy silk panties. *Once and fast* — her Mercedes was probably waiting on the curb. *Once and fast* — her fast-talking boyfriend was probably sitting at the wheel. Smoking? Waiting for his baby?

I fingered her cunt. The cleaved flesh was hairless. One of those women who shaved her pussy. Nothing hidden; no secrets. I had to see. I dropped to my knees and took a good look. The sight of her unadorned pussy — those bare pussy lips — pushed me over the edge. I sank my fingers in as deep as I could go.

Thirty-six. The doors slid open. She was barely damp, and her dryness created an erotic roughness to the fuck. I liked it. She obviously liked it. She was all over me — moaning, making little whimpers.

A few seconds of fingerfucking and she got slick. Still deep inside her, I studied her hairless pussy. Her outer lips were small and girlish. Her clitoris was submerged between them. Obsessed by a need to see, I separated her. At first, her pale pink clit seemed to be a mere flange of skin, but as I stretched her tight, the skin pulled back and a dark red, thick nugget-clit came into view.

"You like it shaved?" she panted.

"So pretty." I began fucking her again. "So pretty." Like a young girl, so soft, so smooth —

I liked her girl-pussy, the strait-laced skirt hiked to her belly, her businesslike demeanor unbuttoned and jerked aside. The doors closed and the car started down. I blindly reached for the buttons but she grabbed my hand.

"Fast," she said, her words moving in like an oncoming storm. "Fast."

Twenty-nine. Twenty-eight. I was running out of time. I pulled her to the floor and climbed on top. I pushed four fingers in and rode her simultaneously. I'd fuck her like she'd never been fucked. Fuck her like she deserved. Seventeen. Sixteen. Fifteen. Fourteen. She clutched my shirt, ripped my sleeve. I rocked her hard and fucked her good. Seven. Six. Five.

She pushed me away. She stood up, adjusted her skirt, buttoned her blouse. She glanced in the mirror and pulled back her hair. Three. Two.

"Can I see you again?" I said quickly.

Before she could answer, the door slid open.

Lobby.

On the other side of the elevator doors, standing with a clipboard in hand, wearing a dressed-for-success business suit and thick-framed glasses, was Sylvia.

"Going up?" she said seductively.

Seemingly flustered, my raven-haired beauty brushed past Sylvia and hurried toward the guard. Sylvia stepped in.

"So sorry to keep you waiting —" She flirtatiously fluttered her eyes. "I know you said eight... Don't you just *hate* when someone's late?"

I ran my hand through my hair, flashed Sylvia a welcome-home smile and pushed Thirty-six.

Up we went.

IF THE SPIRIT MOVES YOU

Woman needed to house-sit the entire
month of March. Live in a quaint cottage,
enjoy privacy and lush green surround-
ings. Great artist's retreat! Must be
reliable and have references.

"Damn."

Rocky tossed the paintbrush to the palette, stuffed
her watercolor-splotched hands into her smock pockets
and stepped back from the canvas. The café scene
still wasn't right. She considered the small figures
huddled around umbrella-shaded tables. Technically,
the painting was exact, yet it lacked that certain
essence of life.

46

Frustration churned in her belly, then radiated up her spine. Another dead end. Where were the flames of inspiration that had once burned so brightly? Where had the depth, the magic, the very soul of her work disappeared to?

With a small inheritance to support her, Rocky had hoped the six months leave from work would fuel her depleted creativity. Ignited by rampant visions of the images she would paint, Rocky had come to San Francisco. She'd electrify crowded cafés with oranges and blues. She'd silhouette sun-soaked skyscrapers in silvers and grays. Splashing pinks and gold, she'd burst sunrises onto unfilled canvases. But instead of the anticipated potpourri of bright, vibrant watercolors, she found the city darkened with endless gray fog and shadowy people.

Rocky's focus drifted from the canvas to her ocean-view window. She could still recall the bold letters of the ad that had led her to this sixth-floor cubbyhole. *Ocean View Studio For Rent.* If she pressed herself against the wall, then yes, she could see past the dirty brick of the adjacent building, across the rooftop to a distant speck of ocean blue. The only thing that had been right about this cramped studio was the rent. In fact, that had been the only right thing about her impulsive move. After six unproductive weeks, her view, her art, her entire life seemed nothing more than a flat, one-dimensional cityscape.

Rocky pulled off her smock and rolled it into a makeshift ball. Aiming for the small table, she made a lay-up shot. It disappeared out the unscreened window.

"Oh great," she muttered, wrestling the sudden urge to fling the palette and easel after it.

She peered out the window, down to the pavement where her paint-splattered smock lay. A scrawny dog trotted from the street, sniffed the smock and raised his leg.

"No! Bad dog!" Rocky yelled helplessly. The dog added a streak of yellow to the multicolored frock. "Goddamned dog."

Rocky slumped into the wooden dining chair and stared vacantly at the repetitive, striped pattern on the dingy curtain. Her spirit was dwindling. Her creative fire sputtered precariously. Desperate to reverse her downward descent, Rocky pressed her forehead against the table and closed her eyes.

In the corner Laundromat, bored with her paperback, Rocky scanned the announcements that were haphazardly pinned to the bulletin board. She had a curious sense that something — not the rooms for rent, not the estate sales, not the reading groups or the free-to-a-good-home dogs — but something on that board held particular significance for her.

She lifted the first layer of notices and did a quick search of those underneath. On a folded piece of notebook paper, the handwritten words, *If The Spirit Moves You,* caught her attention. The letters back-slanted lazily across the thin, blue lines, bringing images of breeze-bowed country grass. An artist's retreat, available the entire month of March — Rocky pulled the notice from the board, stuffed it into her back pocket and headed for the dryer. This was the very thing she needed — a month of privacy, a month of green, a month of creativity. She envisioned herself, on the deck of a small cottage, whirling shades of green on a pearl-white canvas. With brilliant purples and yellows, she'd ignite a field of flowers. Blackbirds' wings would blaze with reds. Burnt-orange butterflies would spiral from leaf-laden trees. The work she could do! The inspiration she'd pluck right from the open skies!

Rocky pulled the crumpled paper from her pocket and read it again. A spontaneous impulse to call immediately — not tonight after more thought, not as soon as she got home, but right that very second — nudged her from the dryers, past the row of washers, to the telephone.

Rocky had never considered crossing the Golden Gate to explore what Marin County had to offer. And now, as she stood on the redwood porch of the cottage, her cottage for the month, she knew that this was the very place she belonged. On top of a grassy hill, guarded by an army of sprawling oaks, the small white house was isolated. Rocky had to park at the end of a long gravel drive, climb three different levels of creaky wooden stairs to reach her refuge. All she brought were her clothes, her CDs, some food and paint supplies. Five trips, up then down, up then down, and she was completely settled. Invigorated by an azure sky and marvelous sunlight, Rocky barely noticed the haul. Within a half-hour, she was already outside, exploring her new place.

The first day, she hiked across the property and

then ventured farther down the backside of the gradually sloping hill. In a green valley, she trampled through overgrown grass, picked bouquets of wildflowers and napped against the stone wall of an abandoned well.

That evening, she did a pencil sketch of the well, an abstract of the trees and a quick-brushed watercolor of a lupine-filled vase. As if guided by a prolific, new muse, Rocky painted late into the night. Eager to capture the polychrome dawn, she was outside, easel upright, palette ready, as early light broke.

By eight a.m., sunrise exploded in dazzling colors across her canvas. With a final stroke, she applied the last mix of orange-pink, then stepped back from her creation. It had substance, it had soul, it had all the deep-reaching qualities she had anxiously deemed lost. Ecstatic, Rocky jumped across the deck, whooping a series of joyful shouts.

Two blue jays briefly stopped quarreling to watch the spectacle below. "I could paint you!" Rocky called to the birds. "Or you!" She pointed to the trees. "Or even you!" She leaned toward a caterpillar that inched its way across the railing.

Artistic energy seemed to hum from every cell. There was so much more she could do, would do! Today, she'd hike back to that deserted well, this time with easel, canvas and paints in tow. Her line drawing was nice, but the prospect of using color — she'd paint the rough, large gray stones that formed its circular wall, the tangles of purple-flowered vines that climbed up and over the border — delighted her.

She'd streak charcoal gray, dab blue-violet and flutter emerald green.

Rocky gathered her gear. She dropped paint tubes and brushes into her large gunnysack. Sketch pad, portable easel, canvas, palette — not wanting to hike back to retrieve a forgotten item, she made sure she had everything she'd need.

She added a thermos of lemonade, some sourdough bread and a soft, woven spread — just in case the urge to nap hit. It was a beautiful spring day and the possibilities were limitless. Out the back, to the valley, toward the well, Rocky trekked.

In several quick drafts, she sketched the well from different perspectives. She sipped lemonade, had a small snack of bread, then drew another, more exact image. The sun was warm, the air fresh, and Rocky, satisfied and content, slipped into an easy sleep.

The valley seemed extraordinarily quiet. Sitting on the blanket, Rocky watched flirtatious butterflies swirl in loops across the fields. She sat in the silence, relishing the focused heat from the overhead sun. A rustling from behind alerted her and she turned, only to discover the image of herself still asleep on the blanket. She was hardly surprised. It was just like her to escape into a dream. She returned her attention to the valley below where a shimmering silhouette, backlighted magnificently by the sun, now stood in the midst of the brilliant green grass.

The figure slowly approached. Her dress, flowing

over her full curves like satin lotion, glimmered. In slow motion, she waved to Rocky. Rocky attempted to raise her arm. How laborious this simple task proved to be. As much as she struggled, her arm seemed too heavy. Instead, Rocky sluggishly nodded.

As if floating across the wildflowers, the woman moved closer. The nearer she came, the more the spring warmth seemed to cool. With intense concentration, Rocky managed to lift her hand to her forehead. Eyes shielded, she squinted. She tried to bring the woman into focus, but the platinum lady emitted a brightness that muted her features.

Up the hill, the transparent figure came — sailing a dream, riding the future. The air chilled further, enveloping Rocky in a pocket of cold. A sudden deep shiver scattered a legion of goose bumps across her flesh.

The woman, trailing a long gown, loomed a few feet from the edge of Rocky's blanket. Her face was hidden behind a draping hood. "I loved to paint." The sound of her words had a muted, under-water quality.

The misty form of the woman drifted back several yards, shimmered like heat waves from a desert road and then slowly returned. As if someone was controlling the scene with a camera lens, the woman gradually came into sharp relief.

She pushed the hood back from her face and gazed wistfully into Rocky's eyes. "Loved, so much, to paint."

The woman had a pale, sad face. Her cinder-gray eyes suggested a restless knowing, as though a century of secrets lurked within. Tinted like the rose quartz Rocky carried in her jacket pocket, the woman's mouth was plush. Rocky could only imagine the provocative words that had been whispered through those lips, could only fantasize the way those lips might feel.

Unexpected yearning hammered at Rocky. As if sensing Rocky's need, the woman squatted at the blanket's edge. But instead of reaching for Rocky, she eased a tube of paint from the gunnysack and squirted purple into her moon-colored hand. A seductive tilt of her shoulder caused the gown's satin strap to slip, revealing a lush, ruby-tipped breast. She smeared the paint across her nipple with a long, sensuous stroke.

Immobilized, Rocky watched the nipple thicken. Like a small, magenta gumdrop, the erect tissue tantalized. Struggling with a suddenly frantic sweet tooth, Rocky stared hungrily at the candy-like nipple. Her mouth watered with hot desire. Her clit hardened with delicious envy.

"Do you like the things I've painted for you?" The woman wiped her hand on Rocky's sketch pad, smearing paint across the penciled flowers. Rocky didn't care. Her only thought was to squeeze the purple-red nipple.

The woman traced the back of Rocky's hand with her fingertip, triggering a penetrating chill up Rocky's arm and through her body. Alarmed by the unnatural coldness of the woman's touch, Rocky instinctively jerked her arm away.

"Do you like the things I've painted for you?" A wintry sadness glazed the woman's words.

Rocky didn't answer and the dream woman began to fade. As if the woman's evanescence and Rocky's perspective were somehow linked, Rocky filled with a gloomy melancholy as the apparition dissolved.

"Don't go," Rocky muttered.

The vanishing woman had dwindled to a silky shadow of white yet Rocky could feel frosty fingers slide across her throat, down to her shoulder, and finally into her bra.

"Just a dream, a cool, cool dream," Rocky murmured as she climbed back into the image of herself, still sleeping peacefully on the blanket. Rocky reached for the woman, but her hands fell through the fading vestige.

Fingers like blue-white ice passed through Rocky's pants and slipped into her sex. Rocky cried in pleasure. Her flesh stung with coldness, burned with coldness. The woman had completely disappeared but her icicle fingers continued to delve further between Rocky's heated lips.

Desperate, Rocky tried to clutch the cool air — trying to find the woman, to grab her, to force those never-melting, piercing fingers deeper. Ice-cold teased her mouth, stiffened her nipples, grazed her belly. The pleasure intensified as a frost-glazed fingertip traveled to the cleave of Rocky's cunt lips. Millimeter by slow millimeter, the finger dipped deeper between the flabby folds.

Rocky could tell that her pussy was hot. She was sure that the heat of her warm-pudding dampness could melt those ice-coated fingers. Cold, streaming drops would race toward her opening, would circle the rim, would drip in — drop by delicious icy drop.

The luminous form of the woman reappeared. "If you stay with me, I'll help you paint. Just like yesterday. Just like today. If you stay with me, you'll always paint."

The image wavered, then dissolved. The sound of

driving rain behind caused Rocky to turn. Farther up the hill, a shower lashed at a grove of baby oaks that surrounded the cottage. Shielding a small canvas from the downpour, a woman hurried to the porch. She stood for a brief moment, flickered into nothing, returned and then was gone. Bewildered, Rocky stared in mute witness to the past — the young trees, the new wood of the cottage, the woman in white standing on the porch.

Rocky quickly turned to the valley. The distant, mature trees stood tall. The butterflies flitted across the field. Again she looked behind her, up the hill. The young trees were gone, replaced by aging, full-grown oaks that completely blocked the view of the old cottage. The rain had stopped, the pocket of cold was gone and the warm sun high in the sky.

Perhaps she had slept a mere ten minutes, perhaps an hour. Groggy, Rocky shaded her eyes and peered toward the sky. Late afternoon. The valley was deserted and remarkably still. For some reason, she had almost expected to see someone waiting for her out in the field. There was a fleeting memory of a dream but she couldn't remember details.

Resting on one elbow, she glanced at the sketch pad that had fallen to her side. Startled, she grabbed the pad. The penciled flowers, interspersed in a maze of dark-lined vines, were now splotched with bright purple paint. Certain she hadn't used any color, she pressed her finger against the plum-tinted petals. The paper was saturated, the paint still wet and a purple smudge smeared her fingertip.

Rocky rummaged through her sack. Canvas, easel, palette. She searched again — canvas, easel, palette. The paints and brushes were gone. A brief inspection around the blanket, under the blanket, to the side, offered no clues. No paints. No brushes.

She recalled gathering the brushes and paints and placing them in the sack. Had she dropped them on the way? She studied the purple-splotched sketch. Could someone have intruded on her seclusion, dabbled with her artwork, then stolen her supplies? She scanned the valley. In the distance, wide-spreading trees blocked her view; behind her, ominous scrubby oaks peered down from the hilltop. Except for the buzzing of nectar-drunk bees, her domain was quiet. Before the nap, the open field had offered a sense of freedom. The knotted oaks had intrigued her. Now, she felt exposed and vulnerable.

Perhaps, on the hike, her paints had dropped from her bag . . .

She stared at the vibrant purple daubed on the canvas.

Or perhaps, she had painted the flowers before the nap and simply forgotten . . .

Then where were brushes? Where were the paints?

She quickly packed her things in the sack. Was there someone watching from the whispering trees ahead? From the twisted trees behind?

With a final, nervous glimpse of the valley, Rocky grabbed the gunnysack and ran home.

As if she hadn't packed them, as if she had inadvertently left them, as if the purple splotches on her sketch had been a figment of her imagination and nothing more — in the cottage, on the coffee table, lay the paint tubes and brushes. Rocky appraised her violet-tipped finger, then pulled the sketch pad from her sack. Lustrous purple was still smeared on the line-drawn flowers.

She squirted a dot of paint on her finger and dabbed it near the already tinted flowers. The wet paint was slightly darker, but even so, Rocky could tell that when the paint dried, the shades would match.

Rocky shifted her focus to the gnarled oaks that hovered out the window of the front room. With dark, rugged bodies and long-reaching arms, the trees knitted a gloomy web. The attempted cheerfulness of the butterscotch-yellow walls did little to distract, nor did the floral curtains. But a glance at the cottage door — the *unlocked* cottage door — snapped Rocky from her middle-of-the-room, statue-like stance. Six fast-steps later, Rocky had that deadbolt secured.

Alert, Rocky leaned against the door. The antique wall clock ticked loudly. Oncoming sunset had abruptly robbed the room of the bit of light the oaks had reluctantly permitted. Muted gray crept in with the shroud of dusk. The curtains fluttered and tiny crystal bells, dangling in the window, tinkled eerily.

A lightning impulse overwhelmed her: *get to the car before dark.* She could be on her way back to the city before the impenetrable night trapped her. Tomorrow, in the daylight, she'd come back for her things.

Go back to the city, and then what? Rocky thought dismally. She may as well throw her easel and paints out the car window on the way home. She took a slow, deep breath. Was this the self-sabotage her therapist had warned her about? Rocky had vehemently protested the suggestion — why would she intentionally conjure up scenarios to inhibit her art, be they subconscious or not? It hadn't made any sense. Yet here she stood, pushed against a locked door, dreading the night.

After tugging off her socks and boots, Rocky surveyed the room. Perhaps a century old, the three-room cottage was an artist's haven. She recalled last evening. The prism-fringed chandelier had glittered with rainbows. The golden-hued walls had enclosed the room like warm, soothing arms. Cluttered with pewter-framed photographs and half-melted candles, the mantelpiece decorated the fireplace like an over-sized charm bracelet. One day at this cottage and her artwork was the best it had been in the last few years. She was inspired like never before, burning with an internal fire that kept her painting late into the night. It was as if a stirring, powerful magic had come into Rocky — into this cottage, late in the night — and guided her strokes, conjuring master-pieces. She would not give up, not this time.

Barefoot, Rocky headed to the window. The miniature glass bells no longer clinked. The curtains were still. Menacing figures only minutes before, the trees were now simply trees. How subtly her mind had distorted her perception. In the blink of an eye, a clump of old trees had mutated from protective to threatening. And this afternoon, in a panic, she had run home — uphill the entire way — from what? The elusive remnants of a dream? Purple splotches on a sketch pad? And what of the splotches? Now that she had a moment for rational thought, events seemed less bizarre. The unsolicited purple was probably the free-lance work of a mischievous prankster. She should know better than to nap in a field.

The coolness of the hardwood floor soothed her tired feet. Last night the cottage was cold. Tonight, she'd build a fire. The vision of her easel, set up in front of roaring flames, excited her.

"Self-sabotage," Rocky said to no one but herself.

Filled with the relief self-knowing brings, she unlocked the deadbolt. On the side of the house, where the trees were just trees, the wood was piled. Tonight, with a fire burning bright, she'd paint ravishing purple flowers interlaced with green vines. Nothing could stop her now.

Firelight flickered on the walls as the last log danced with flames. Rocky studied the intricate weaving of flowers and vines on her canvas. She daubed a brush-tip of violet several more times, one more touch of royal blue and then stretched.

She had been sitting at the easel for . . . ? She lifted her abandoned wristwatch from the floor. It was almost midnight. After another stretch, this time long and deep, she climbed from the stool. With one wandering glance from the canvas, Rocky became acutely aware of the surrounding dark room. Near the kitchen, the obscured form of the overstuffed chair hunched like a grotesque predator. The antique floor lamp, tall and graceful by day, stood by the chair like a rough-looking stranger. From a night-black corner came the lonely ticking of the wall clock. Like that of a despairing heart, the empty rhythm persisted.

Tick tock. Tick tock. Tick tock.

The house was still . . . or was it? Rocky concentrated. A sporadic creaking, just outside the window, was barely discernible. Was it simply the wind grating the branches, or someone stealing across the porch? *She had locked the door, hadn't she?*

A dull thud sounded behind her. Startled, Rocky spun around. In the fireplace, the charred log had fallen. In three fast steps, Rocky crossed the room and had the ceiling light switched on. The chandelier's prisms showered tiny rainbows across the walls. Like light-driven bats, the shadows had disappeared — in the corner slumped the old chair, by its side stood the elegant lamp.

In the center of the room, befriended by light, Rocky listened intently. Except for the crackling fire, the house was quiet once again. Rocky waited. Not even the slightest creak could be heard. The auditory mirages that the darkness had brought had slithered out with the shadows.

Yes, the door was locked. Yes, the house was safe. Rocky turned off the light and headed for bed.

Rocky clicked on the nightstand light and glanced around the room. On the antique bureau, an array of cut-glass perfume bottles sparkled on an oval, mirrored platform. Carved miniature cherubs smiled from the armoire door. The emerald-hued comforter that lay plush on the double bed accentuated the green leaves spiraling throughout the floral wallpaper pattern.

Above the bureau, a long rectangular window spanned the bedroom wall. When closed and clasped, the large wooden shutters provided privacy, but the small room suffered. Unclasped and swung open, as they were now, the shutters seemed to hold back the confining walls, giving the illusion of space.

A slight rasping from somewhere outside sent an immediate alarm through Rocky. Her attention darted back to the window but the room's reflection in the glass obstructed her view. Earlier, when the day was bright, she had relished the large, uncovered window. Now, as she stood in the doorway wondering what lurked in the blackness beyond, she regretted the open shutters.

Close the shutters now! The cherubs screamed silently from the armoire door. The room seemed suddenly smaller, as if swallowed into itself, leaving only the vast, threatening window.

Rocky slammed the shutters, leapt into bed and yanked the blanket over her head. Under the protection of the comforter, Rocky promised herself a return to therapy as soon as she could afford it.

A pounding on the door jerked Rocky from a deep, hard sleep. She pitched forward in bed. Her heart thumped. Her breath was short. She sat, alert, not moving. An unsettling stillness oozed throughout the house.

"Who's there?" Her voice broke the silence.

Three loud thumps came — from the front room?

the kitchen? Rocky wasn't sure. She pulled the blanket around her but something tugged it back down. Again she jerked the blanket then clicked on the light in one fast move. There was no one else in the room.

She heard a clock being wound, then silence. Something crashed to the floor. Silence again. A chair scraped across the hardwood floor.

"What do you want?" Rocky called. Was there someone in the house or was this a dream, like this afternoon. If she twisted around, right this instant, would she discover herself still sleeping soundly?

Prepared to find herself lying in bed, prepared to fall back into the dream — Rocky quickly turned. Except for two feather pillows, the bed was unoccupied. As if she could sense that it was waiting for her, as if she knew all along, Rocky glanced from the lace-trimmed pillows to the flower-patterned wall. In runny purple paint that streaked down the wall haphazardly, the words — *Do you like the things I've painted for you* — were scrawled.

"Oh God —" Rocky felt paralyzed. An intense icy fear burned through her.

In the front room, things began smashing to the floor. This was not a dream — someone was definitely in the house.

"Oh shit," Rocky whispered frantically. "Shit. Shit. Shit." She climbed out of bed, scanned the room for a makeshift weapon and grabbed an umbrella. "I don't want to go in there. I don't want to go in there," Rocky muttered. Umbrella raised like a sword, she reluctantly headed toward the unknown.

Set to lunge into the darkness, primed to strike —

62

no matter the cost, Rocky crouched in the doorway. She listened carefully. The house reverberated with a deadening silence.

"Who's there?" She peered into the front room. Nothing.

"I've got a weapon," Rocky threatened.

She waved the umbrella, hurried to the adjacent wall and switched on the chandelier. Light filled the room. The chair had been moved several feet from the floor lamp. The easel was near the window. Except for one photograph still on the mantel, all the frames and candles had been knocked to the floor.

"I've got a weapon," Rocky called again. She tiptoed to the kitchen, then the bath. She checked the closets, one by one. The deadbolt was still locked, the windows secured. Umbrella raised, Rocky turned a slow circle, scanning the front room one last time.

Positioned dead-center above the fireplace, the lone photograph seemed to glimmer like an eerie beacon. Rocky stepped through the clutter of candles and frames to the pewter-framed picture. The aged black-and-white portrait was lined with thin, white cracks. Three young women, dressed in high-necked blouses and ankle-length skirts, stood on the cottage steps. Rocky traced her finger across the face of the center woman who stared into the camera. Her wistful, sad gaze looked strangely familiar. Rocky studied the woman's features, certain she had seen cinder-gray eyes and rose quartz-colored lips just like them somewhere before.

"Do you like the things I've painted for you?"

Rocky spun around. The woman from the photograph stood boldly in the bedroom doorway.

"Who the hell are you? What do you want!"
Words flew from Rocky without thought. She held the
umbrella high.

"To paint. Through you." The woman in white
stepped closer and a sudden coldness seeped from the
floor toward the ceiling. As if riding the slow wave of
chilled air, the scent of lavender permeated the room.

"To paint?" Rocky's heart thumped madly as she
scrutinized the woman. Violet paint spotted the bodice
of her gown and covered her pale hands.

In a slow, mesmerizing movement, the woman
lowered the straps of her satin dress. Like thick
cream pouring from a pitcher, the gown rippled down
her voluptuous curves to the floor. She stepped even
closer, retrieved a tube of paint from the palette and
squirted more purple into her palm.

Rocky stared greedily at the woman's pert breasts.
Her nipples were like large rubies. Rocky fought the
impulse to run her thumb over their perfect square-
cut shape.

"I loved to paint." The woman smeared the scoop
of paint across her breast, smothering her gem-hard
nipple in a flood of violet.

Rocky could hear the low, slapping sound as the
woman lazily squished the paint against her flesh.
Stroking each breast, then drifting down her slightly
rounded belly, the woman continued to spread the
paint. The deep violet contrasted sharply with her
moonlight skin and recklessly emphasized her
honey-hued triangle of hair.

Hypnotized by the flirty pink flesh that dangled
between the slender lips, Rocky did not move. She
watched the woman push the paint, in fuller strokes,

up to her erect nipples, then down to the nest of golden hair.

The woman's paint-stained finger slipped between the folds of pussy flesh. With snap-like strokes she nudged her clit back and forth, back and forth until her entire hand beat in fast-paced circles.

"*I* excite you. *I* ignite you. *My* fire allows you to paint," the woman murmured. In a fast motion, she cleaved her lips, exposing the hidden treasures. Her purple-tinted clit hung like a tiny bunch of juicy grapes.

Rocky stared at the lush, fruit-like cluster. Surprisingly dry and parched, her mouth clamored for relief. How desperately she craved a simple suck from that wine-soaked clitoris! She'd bury her face in that Burgundy oasis. Immersed in a bacchanalian orgy, she'd guzzle the gods' sweet nectar until she fell to the floor, drunk and satiated. *Excite? Ignite?* Isn't that what the woman had offered to do? Well, then yes, Rocky thought eagerly. Yes. Yes. Yes, yes, yes!

A mischievous smile illuminated the woman's face. "Yes?" she asked, as if she had heard Rocky's thoughts.

Delirious, Rocky dropped the umbrella and stumbled toward the woman. She'd lick, then suckle that clump of meaty grapes. She'd show this woman a thing or two about fire-starting.

The light from the chandelier flickered, faded, then finally was gone. For a brief moment, the muted glow from the bedroom dimly lit the front room, then the entire house fell into complete darkness.

"Hey!" Nipples throbbing, clit aching, Rocky cursed her sudden blindness. "Where are you?"

"Would you follow me into the dark for the fire?" The woman's sultry words teased from behind.

Rocky did a fast pivot. Hide and seek. Hide and fucking seek, she thought. Crazy with passion, she reached her hands into the darkness ahead, taking one small step. Even with no lights, she'd find the woman, have the woman. With one of her thick, stiff paint brushes, she'd stroke the woman's pulpy clit. Over and over that unyielding brush tip would tickle and tease the flaccid, bulbous flesh.

The image of her brush on the woman's clitoral sack was clear in Rocky's mind. With the slightest amount of pressure, Rocky would cause the brush tip to fan out. The tissues would tighten into a hardened, rigid shaft and Rocky would rotate the spread brush in slow, delicious circles. And then —

"Would you follow me into the darkness?" the woman whispered in Rocky's ear. Her cold fingers tightened around Rocky's wrist. "Yes or no?"

The hot desire racing in Rocky's blood overshadowed the surge of cold. All that mattered was *this* moment and that woman. "Yes," Rocky stammered.

The woman pulled Rocky across the black room. Rocky stumbled over the clutter but the woman's strength kept her from falling to the floor. The deadbolt turned, the front door creaked open, and into the night the woman led Rocky.

As though riding an icy breeze, they soared through the oaks and down the hill, finally stopping at the abandoned stone well.

Still clutching Rocky's wrist, the paint-splattered woman climbed on the edge of the well. "In here," she pleaded. "Follow me and we'll paint forever."

"Are you crazy!" Rocky shouted, struggling to pull her hand from the woman's tight grip. The woman was strong and refused to let go. Rocky frantically wrestled, until a vigorous shove freed her but sent the woman, thrown off-balance, plunging into the well.

The sliver of moon hung in the black sky like a dimly lit sickle. There were no stars. The air was brisk. An eerie quiet shuddered through the valley and out into the unknown.

Rocky peered into the well's abyss. "Are you okay?"

Silence.

She leaned way over the edge. "Are you okay?"

From behind, strong hands slammed against Rocky's back and she tumbled into the well.

"Somebody, please help me!" Rocky screamed, lunging forward. The house was quiet. The bedroom was dark. She clicked on the light, leapt out of bed and went directly to the front room. The pictures still lined the mantel. The easel and chair were right where she had left them. An ash-white log smoldered in the fireplace.

Relieved, she returned to the bedroom but froze in the doorway. On the wall, above the bed, the haunting words still remained. Rocky was out of there by morning.

After three unproductive weeks back in the city, Rocky fell into a grim depression. No matter what she did or where she went, she wasn't able to paint. Dreamless nights melted into art-less days. Restless, anguished and uninspired, Rocky sat in her studio for hours at a time, staring blankly at an empty canvas.

After days of feeling hopeless and desperate, Rocky took a drive over the Golden Gate. Perhaps if she just sat in that field for one half day, she'd be able to paint once again.

With paint gear in tow, she hiked back to the old well. The midday sun was high in the sky. A scattering of bees dipped in and out of the profluent blossoms that bordered the well.

After several unsuccessful hours in front of her easel, Rocky felt even worse. Would she never paint again? Restless, Rocky leaned over the edge of the well and peered in.

"Hello?" Rocky called.

After the remarkable rush of inspiration she had experienced during her stay at the cottage, she could no longer tolerate her vapid, one-dimensional life. It was obvious — there was nothing left if she could not paint. No reason to go back to the city, no reason for anything.

"I've changed my mind," Rocky said calmly into the musky darkness. An apologetic edge shadowed her words.

The afternoon sun was in its descent and the air was beginning to cool. On the rim of the old stone well, Rocky swung her legs across the abyss and waited for the spirit to move her.

> **GENEROUS REWARD**
>
> for the return of a dark brown,
> leather-bound journal. Lost in the vicinity
> of Bette's Books & Café. Has a brass clasp
> and the initials T.Z. imprinted in gold on
> front. Sentimental value.

I found the book under the table, shoved in the corner against the wall. It was bound in expensive leather with the letters *T.Z.* inscribed in gold in the lower right-hand corner. The contents were private — the brass, locked clasp made that point quite clear.

My initial response was to turn the book over to Bette. She managed the café — shit, in her own way, Bette managed the entire women's community. If anyone could find the book's rightful owner, it was Bette. She was sitting on the counter, talking on the phone. With the wave of a hand, I could have called her over. Hell, even with her back turned, Bette saw everything that went on. A quick nod would get her attention and she'd be at my table, taking the book . . . I could have handed it to her or left the book on the table. Instead — and I swear to God, I don't know why — I slipped the book into my briefcase and hurried out the door.

I pulled the book from my briefcase and tossed it on the bed. What the hell had gotten into me? Tomorrow, first chance I had, I'd relinquish the goods to Bette. The dark leather seemed to float in the cushiony thickness of my sea-blue comforter. Light from the bedside lamp glimmered in the gold letters and danced across the brass lock.

I shifted my focus to the Stephen King novel on the nightstand. Minutes from now, I'd be in my sweats, in bed, immersed in *The Shining*. I un-buttoned my shirt — my gaze returning to the flashy clasp. What could be so secret that it had to be kept under lock and key? Jeans off, sweatpants on — was there any private matter in this town that Bette didn't know about, hell, that all of us didn't already know about?

I stared at the flamboyant barrier and suddenly understood. It was that lock — that arrogant, cocksure lock — that had forced me to bury the book in my briefcase and sneak it back to my house. *Bet you'd never have the guts to jimmy the lock and find out what's so damn personal,* the haughty, shiny clasp had subtly challenged then . . . and now.

"Yeah, right," I smirked.

I caught my hard-set expression in the mirror and broke into a laugh. Trying to top a goddamned lock? Shit, my life was taking a serious nosedive. I grabbed the book, set it on the dresser and climbed into bed. Tomorrow, the book was going to Bette.

In bed, in the dark, I tried to relax. There was something about that book that nagged at me. Ten minutes passed. Fifteen minutes passed. Something about that lock that aggravated the hell out of me. Sixteen minutes. Seventeen. I switched on the light.

Told you so, the lock mocked.

"The hell you did," I muttered, climbing out of bed.

I tried to pull the pages open, to peek inside the book, but the leather strap, secured by the fastened lock, wouldn't permit the slightest gap. I scanned the room for a tool. Surely I'd never infringe on someone's privacy — certainly I'd never cross that line. It was the high-skilled challenge of opening a locked clasp that intrigued me — a butch sort of thing, a mechanical contest. I was an innocent victim of the simple, human desire to be the best that I could be.

I dug into the keyhole with a metal nail file until it clicked. The strap loosened without a hitch and the leather-bound book fell open.

I suppose it's wrong for me to feel this way but I can't seem to break the cycle.

Handwritten words filled the page. Impulsively, I

slammed the book shut. I felt dirty. I felt slimy. Reading a stranger's diary — it was disgustingly wrong . . . and yet . . . an overwhelming, involuntary reflex forced me — against my will — to open that book and read on.

Last night, I didn't care. For a few moments, I pretended I was L. and squeezed my thighs together the way she tightens hers when she comes. Something about being her aroused me incredibly. I visualized her face — and I was her. I imagined her hard nipples — and I was her. I was me, running my hand over her belly. I was her, feeling my firm caress. I pinched her protruding nipples, I teased her swollen clit, yet I was her, squirming on the bed, moaning in pleasure. Within seconds, I was over the edge. I came so intensely that I wet the bed.

With a fast, abrupt jerk, I closed the book. Guilt scrambled through me but was instantly chased off by the more pressing question — who the hell was L.?
I flipped the book open.

L. said she'd come over tonight. I waited until eleven for her call. I hate when she says she's coming and doesn't show. I cried until I fell asleep, vowing never to see her again. A purring sound outside my window woke me. The digital clock blared a red, two forty-five. I peeked between the curtains and there she was, sitting on the fence, meowing like a cat. I just stared at her, torn between anger and desire. God, how many times she's put me in that place!
Dressed in black, perched on that fence like a

sleek, smooth tomcat, she flashed me her I-know-you're-mad-but-let-me-in-anyway smile. As if in a trance, as if I had never cried a single tear, I hurriedly opened the window. She climbed in, smelling like whiskey and stale cigarettes — it didn't matter, not in that moment, not while she was smothering me with hot kisses and whispered intent.

She made love to me fast and hard. Against the wall, she pushed me, drove her fingers into me, slammed me. It was wild and rough, the way we both needed it. She pounded into me over and over and I came, just from the way the cold wall felt against my back. I bit her several times, I think . . . I'm not sure, I was set on fire and uncontainable. I hope to hell J. doesn't see those bite marks . . . or do I?

I laid the journal on my lap. Christ, L. was skating on thin ice, that's for sure — climbing in and out windows, risking bite marks. I leaned back in the bed and imagined hanging on Melissa's fence and meowing like a cat. Would she think I was out of my mind or would she open her window, invite me in and let me fuck her hard. I rubbed my shoulder as if the bite marks already stung the flesh. The demanding urge to dress in black and head for Melissa's overtook me. I threw aside the comforter and sat on the edge of the bed, reconsidering my options. Climb on her fence? Knowing Melissa, she'd shoot first, ask questions later. I visualized being dragged with a bullet wound in the shoulder to a waiting ambulance.

"What the hell were you thinking?" Melissa would be crying.

"She's nuts," Melissa's girlfriend for the night would mutter. "Full moon and your ex turns into were-cat."

I thought of the bullet, grimaced and rubbed my shoulder one last time. "Were-cat, my ass," I mumbled, reluctantly tucking myself back into bed. I lifted the journal . . .

We had a date at her house. When I arrived, a sealed envelope with my name scribbled on it was tacked to the door. Wasn't she home? Had she canceled our date? My stomach plunged to the ground. I ripped open the envelope. Inside was a note — Door's open. Come in — and a thin joint.

I went back to my car. Normally, I wouldn't smoke pot. I took the joint from the envelope and sniffed it. Normally, I wouldn't do half the things I do for L. I scanned the neighborhood, lit the joint then scrunched in the front seat. I took a puff.

Instantly light-headed, flighty and high, I fluttered from the car to her porch. The front door opened to a darkened hall. I stood in the doorway, listening to the hypnotic beat of a drum. Dim light flickered from the living room. Slow steps — I followed the drumming. Slow steps, I followed the light.

L. was in the center of the room. Wearing only a leather thong, she did a slow, sensuous dance to the erotic drumbeat. Like an undulating cobra, she twisted and turned. Her body, lean and muscular, excited me. It would have been enough to only watch her move. I could have masturbated, brought myself off, just from the way her thighs tightened, just from the way her curved ass swayed.

Surrounded by baskets and ceramic pots, she

danced on a large, woven mat. An exotic scent —
perhaps spices from the East — filled the room. A
coiling ribbon of smoke curled from behind the large
palm. In the corner, partially hidden by the plant, a
masked woman rhythmically thumped a pot-shaped
drum.

L. swirled in slow circles. Her hips rotated, teased,
tempted. The mystical perfume thickened the air and I
felt suddenly faint. The pulse of the drumming
quickened. L.'s eyes burned like an untamed
predator's. One sultry glance from her could transport
me around the world. Tonight, I sped through the
night, deep into a tangled jungle. That's where she
took me. That's where we went.

L. began to move in wild, erratic steps. The
spinning scents twirled with her and I became
disoriented and dizzy. The palm reeled, first in a
slow, big circle, then faster, even faster. I was
confused — was there one palm? Two palms? Three?

The drumbeat intensified. Deep in the jungle, dark
in the night-large cats peered through the foliage.
Lightning-fast tigers, slinking panthers watched
between the leaves. L. gyrated and the room whirled.

Into the jungle of desire we descended. L. fell to
her knees and dipped her hands into a large ceramic
bowl. In a sharp, dramatic motion, she lifted her
hands toward the ceiling. Clear liquid streamed down
her arms. She smeared her breasts, her belly, her legs
with the glistening fluid. She stood up, began dancing
once again.

To a candelabra, she glided. She swirled her hands
over the flame, all the while staring intently at me.
A flash leapt to her fingertips, flared momentarily,
then disappeared. I watched in awe. Again she dipped

her hands in the bowl, spilled the liquid down her body and returned to the candles.

She whisked her hands through the lights and several erratic sparks jumped to her fingers. Down her taut body, she ran her hands. Her flame-charged fingers kissed the shimmering moisture and fiery streaks rippled across her flesh. Her nipples squeezed into dark pillars. Over and over, she rolled the fire across her breasts and belly. I felt each sting of heat. I felt each yellow-blue wave.

Her swollen clit glittered from her coal-black sex hair like a ruby flare. I took a step, I came in closer. And the drumming was good. The throbbing was better. I walked across the mat and into the center. I reached for L. I reached for the heat. She was slippery, slick, wet and hot. She ripped at my blouse. I tore at my pants. And the drummer was thrumming. The drummer was pounding.

"Oh yes," I pleaded.

"Oh yes," she begged.

Into the liquid, she dipped her fingers. Across my hungry breasts, she smeared the fuel. The strong scent of rubbing alcohol surrounded me along with her heat. Just her look, just her touch, could set me ablaze. My nipples quivered. My pussy ached.

Flames danced on her fingers, disappeared, then returned. She raced the fiery tips through the air. Walking toward me, coming for me. Would it burn? Would it sting? Would it singe? Would it sear?

I took a deep breath, I let out a shrill cry. And the drumming went on and on and on. Waves of heat tickled, sizzled and stung. My pussy was soaked. Cream slid down my thigh. God, I ignited for her, blazed for her, burned.

I dropped the journal with a gasp. Who the hell were these women? I did a quick mental scan of the group who hung out at the café. No one I knew played with this kind of fire. I glanced at the clock. Eleven forty-five. Would Bette be awake? I threw off the blanket again and climbed out of bed. I rummaged through my briefcase for my phone book but it was a book of matches that I pulled out.

The crazy idea hit hard, then took over. Into the bathroom, I sprinted. I grabbed a bottle of rubbing alcohol and dipped my finger in. The match lit with a hiss. The fire was small. I waved my finger above the flame. First six inches from the heat, then five, four inches, then three. I moved my finger aside and appraised the flame one last time — that cruel, hot flame. Didn't seem like this was going to be a real fun time, no sir, not to me. I flipped the burning match into the toilet and flushed it fast. Those women were nuts.

Back in bed, I dropped T.Z.'s journal to the floor and clicked off the light. Eleven fifty-three. Eleven fifty-four. Eleven fifty-five. The image of the women, dancing with fire, was crystal clear. I could hear the drums. I could hear their moans.

I sat back up and turned on the light. The broken lock glared at me. *See? I told you so.*

Without another thought, I grabbed the journal.

L. says she has a lot to sort through. That her and J. are having some problems. She's so secretive about what's really going on between the two of them. I wonder if J. saw the bite marks???

I was in the café today. It's a good place to write. I don't have to worry about being bothered since I'm certain L. won't come there. I keep thinking that the best way to get over her is to meet someone new, but it's ludicrous to think I'd ever meet anyone as exciting as L.

"Hello, Bette?" I ran my hand through my hair. "I hope I didn't wake you."

"That's okay, just dozing off." Bette sounded groggy.

"It's Jackie. I'm sorry, really — it's just that —"

"Are you okay?" Bette seemed more awake.

I studied the journal on my lap. T.Z.'s Journal. Our journal — after all, didn't T.Z. and I share a certain intimacy at this point? I already had formed a definite disliking for L. She cheated, she lied, she had no regard, no respect for T.Z. or for J. The thought of T.Z. falling in any deeper bothered me. If I read more of the journal, got to know more about T.Z. — perhaps I could help her untangle from L.?

"Are you okay?" Bette repeated.

If I said that I had the journal, Bette would expect me to turn it in. Instinctively, I covered the leather book with my hand. Damn. Why hadn't I thought this through before I impulsively made the call.

"Sure," I answered off the cuff. "Was just wondering how you were."

"You saw me tonight, Jackie. About two hours ago. I was fine then, I'm fine now." I could hear the suspicious tone in her voice.

"Good . . . good . . ." I said the words real slow, trying to drag out the reply until I came up with a somewhat reasonable excuse for the after-midnight intrusion.

"Is this about Lissa?" Bette said casually. "After all, she was in today, with someone — a new girl in town, quite attractive. As much as I'm not one to gossip about these things —"

"No," I cut in. "I could care less about Melissa." God, I hated when they called her Lissa, when they brought her up, when they forced her back into my life. Melissa was nowhere and everywhere since she walked out my door. A familiar emptiness swept through me.

"Then, what the hell's up with you?" Bette said firmly.

Less than two weeks and Melissa was already in the café with another woman, already the talk of the town. Goddamn her. I should go to her house. I should go to her house, sit on her fence, meow a few times and break up her party. Let her shoot first, let them drag me away! I'll give the town something to gossip about.

I pictured Melissa sitting at a table, laughing it up — like I should be doing, like I could be doing, if I played my cards right.

"Speaking of the café..." I kept my voice cool. "Earlier today, there was a woman sitting at corner table. She was alone, writing in a journal." I glanced at the sentence, that sentence... *the best way to get over her is to meet someone new*... "Who is she, Bette? I figured, if anyone would know, it would be you."

"I didn't see you earlier," Bette said carefully.

"I was just passing by, took a glimpse in the window and there she was." I held my breath. *C'mon, give me a break here, Bette.*

"I really don't like to get involved in —"

Since when? I whispered, "Just a name, Bette."

"And you won't say I told you?" Bette said, her voice tight. "I've got a business to run. I try to stay out of personal dynamics."

Yeah, right, I thought. *Give me the goods, Bette.*

"Of course not, Bette. I just want to have a little talk with her — get to know her — surely you can under- stand. What with the breakup with Melissa and all, I just want to —"

"Okay, okay, I get it," Bette interrupted. "Her name is Tasia. She rarely comes into the café. That's all I know. The rest is up to you. But I'm certain that it's best —"

Distracted by the rhythmic sound of her name — Tasia, Tasia, Tasia — I was bombarded by visions of her and me, naked, blazing, dancing in my front room. The intensity of the drumbeat thickened, drowning out Bette's monotone voice.

I'd dip my fingers in alcohol. I'd pour the cool liquid down her shoulder, to her breast. Her nipple would clench to a tight red stone. A trail of sparks from my fingers to her tit, from my fingers to her round belly, from my fingers to her milk-dew clit — I'd start fires that couldn't be stopped. She'd ignite for me. She'd flare. I'd treat her right. I'd do her good.

I could see her on the floor, on the table, on the bed. Her legs were stretched wide, with me between them. I'd grab my dildo and warm it, warm it, warm it. Under steamy water, I'd run it, soak it. She likes

80

it hot? She'd get it hot. Oh yes. Oh yes. I'd jiggle the dildo in her cunt, pluck it out. Slice it in, snap it out.

I could see her pussy — drooling, mouthing, sucking on that heated spear. I'd tease the lips. I'd tug her lips. I'd pump her clit and sink the stick and —

"— you *do* agree, don't you?" The sharpness of Bette's words cut like a machete through my jungle of fantasy.

Agree? Agree? What wasn't there to agree to? "Sure," I muttered. I was ready to hang up, needed to hang up.

"Can I go back to sleep now?"

"Yeah, thanks," I muttered. Tasia had a fleshy fat clit. I could see it. I could see it all.

"Anytime," Bette replied.

Tasia. Tasia. Tasia. I felt wired. I felt electric. I felt plugged in and unable to stop. My body hummed with the need for release. I grabbed the journal and haphazardly flipped through the pages for something to sink my teeth into while I worked my pussy off.

She walked in, already aroused. Her eyes seared. Her tongue repeatedly slid across her full lips, making them damp, keeping them moist.

"I got something special for you," she said.

She clicked off the overhead light, switched on a flashlight and led me to the dining room table.

God, I love how she's so confident, so certain. She's a genie, a purveyor of fantasy. Sex with L. is like soaring on a magic carpet to exotic lands. I wondered what she had in store, where she'd take me next.

"Lie down." Her words were muffled beneath her hard breath.

The beam of light haphazardly jumped across the walls as she helped me onto the table. She raised my skirt to my waist and pulled my panties off.

"I've been hot for you all day." She pulled something from her jacket. "It's a drinking flask. Bought it today at the Renaissance Faire." She held it in the stream of light. Molded in successive curves that resembled a large helping of swirled, soft-serve ice cream, the glass glittered.

"What I do, is this —" She screwed the glass flask onto the lit end of the flashlight. "It's a perfect fit. Like it was made for this very thing. Let those fifteenth-century folks eat, drink and be merry — I've got better ideas for their hand-blown flasks."

She spread the lips of my pussy. "Okay, sugar, okay, sweet, let me show you how this works." The smooth tip of the dildo-like glass was pressed against my opening. My clitoris, my lips, every private crevice, every secret fold was illuminated. "Can I spotlight your pussy and show you off?"

I stared down at the flashlight between my legs. I'd never seen anything so incredibly erotic.

"Can I show you off?" she said again.

"Can she?" Three women came into the room and stood behind L. I'd never seen them before and had no idea who they were.

"Isn't she pretty? Doesn't she have the prettiest

pussy you've ever seen?" L. jimmied the tip against the borders of my slit.

Like a pink butterfly preparing for flight, my lower lips rested on the curved glass. L. popped the end into my opening and the flappy lips wrapped around the radiant dildo. She pushed in, then out. Smearing a streak of white with each stroke, the lips rode the glass.

"A pretty, pretty pussy. Have a look. See how she's seeping? See how we've got her milked up?"

The women stepped closer. One squeezed my nipples while the others spread my lips so tight that I whimpered with pleasure.

L. continued to slow-fuck me with the glass tool. Using a long, delayed motion, she screwed it in. Each successive ring — larger and bulkier than the last — burrowed its way in farther. I felt stretched. I felt clamped open. The flask corkscrewed in, then rolled out. And that light, oh that delicious, focused light made my pussy seem so red, so hard, so ready. Like a shiny, claret pendant, my wedge of flesh glistened for all to see.

They held me like that forever. They fucked me and fucked me and fucked me so good. Over and over — and my pussy thickened. Over and over — and my pussy sucked like a baby does a teat. The clear glass became frosty, sugar-coated with my juice. In the light, the white creamed from my lips and swirled on the flask. L. dabbed her finger in the dew and tapped it across my blood-flushed teardrop of a clit.

L. spiraled the dildo in and out and fingered my clit simultaneously. A finger artist, a pussy-master, *she flicked me off. The women watched. The women helped. The glass got whiter. My pussy got redder. Everyone was moaning and whimpering and panting. We climbed on a magic carpet — she and I and them — and we raced in fast circles around the world.*

I threw the book aside. I needed both hands now. One to hold my cunt apart, the other to stir my clit. Those women were wild, over the edge. Tasia. Tasia. Tasia. Where are you now? I nudged my rock-hard clit back and forth, while visions of her, of me, of them, of us — soaring across the skies — cascaded through my mind.

I woke up, awkwardly hugging the open journal. Several pages were crinkled and creased. Flattening them as best I could, I shut the diary. I managed to cram the clasp back together although the lock itself no longer worked.

All I could think of was Tasia. I wanted to meet her, to protect her and goddamnit, to have her! Had I ever been with someone as experimental as Tasia? Melissa was always too busy at night school, too tired from her job, too PMS to give me that kind of a shot.

Perhaps if I had been more . . . ? I considered my fleeting urge last night to race to her house, to climb onto her fence. Would an impulsive act like that have sparked Melissa's passion for me?

I laid the journal on the floor and stepped onto the leather cover. Balanced on one foot, I closed my eyes and imagined the crumpled diary pages smooth and unwrinkled.

Had I somehow let Melissa down?

I turned the journal over and climbed back on.

Could I have somehow averted her abrupt disinterest in sex?

"It's not you," she had said. "It's me. Some kind of a lesbian no-sex phase."

I caught a glimpse of myself in the mirror. Although at that moment I looked slightly ridiculous — perched on a book at seven a.m. — I had flair. I had style. And with a broad-minded woman like Tasia, I could have a lot, lot more.

I'd sneak the journal back into the café, stuff it in the same corner I'd found it in — and wait. Sooner or later, Tasia would show. She likes confidence? A woman who's certain? Hell, I could do it all.

I showered, doused myself in Guess for Men and headed for brunch at Bette's café.

With a double *latte* and a scone, I waited. I was in the corner, the journal was in place and everything was set. I'd be confident, I'd be certain, I'd be what she wanted and more.

If I had been these things with Melissa?

A sudden flash of Melissa and her new woman came to mind — tête à tête at Bette's Café, making a spectacle for all to see. *Is this about Lissa? After all, she was in today with someone new* . . . Even groggy from sleep, Bette managed to spread the hot-off-the-press gossip.

Melissa, calling herself "Lissa" again — carefree, single and available. Shit. Only two weeks out of her relationship with me. Fine. Let Melissa have her girlfriend. Let Melissa have it all. I had my own life now. I had Tasia. Tasia. Tasia. I tried to imagine her. Was she dark-skinned and exotic? Fair and creamy? Was she thin and small-breasted? Full and voluptuous? It didn't matter, really, we were way beyond that.

Bette hadn't shown yet — just as well. The last thing I wanted was ol' hungry eyes devouring every bit of gossip she could squeeze from my life. Melissa had already spoon-fed her appetizers, and my frantic midnight call had no doubt fanned the flame for the entrée.

Flames. The thought revived images of Tasia and L. in a frenzied, erotic dance. I stared at the door. Ten minutes. Twenty minutes. An hour passed. No one came in to search the corner. I peered at *The Shining* without retaining a single word.

The lunch crowd filtered in. I ordered a burger. I reread chapter ten.

"Hi, Jackie." Melissa stood at the table with a handful of fliers. "How've you been?"

The nauseating vision of Melissa, sitting in the café with her new girl, quickly came to mind. I shrugged and looked back at my book.

"Are you still angry about us?" She sat across from me.

"About us? There is no *us*. Two weeks apart and you've already got a new woman," I blurted. "Lucky, lucky you."

Melissa lay her things on the table and reached for my hand. "I'm just trying to fill the vacant hours."

"Right." Not wanting to give her the luxury of reading the pain in my eyes, I stared at the pile of fliers. *Generous Reward* caught my attention.

"What did you lose?" Grateful to change the subject, I tugged a flier off the top of the pile.

"My friend lost her —"

Melissa's words were drowned in the roaring rush of blood to my face. Each word stung my eyes as I read. *A leather-bound book. A leather-bound, brass-clasped book with the initials T.Z.* Tasia's book. My book.

Without thinking, I lunged across the table and grabbed Melissa's shirt. "Tasia? Tasia? You're fucking around with Tasia?"

"How do you know about Tasia?" Melissa stammered, pulling my hands away.

"How do I know about Tasia?" I was out of control. Melissa and Tasia? Melissa and Tasia? A sudden image of Melissa, three weeks ago, came to mind. "Where'd you get those?" I had asked, pointing to several bruises on her arm. "Walked into a metal thing at work," she had said vaguely. The words from the journal came fast and hard — *I bit her several times, I think ... I'm not sure, I was set on fire and uncontainable. I hope to hell J. doesn't see those bite marks ... or do I?*

Melissa and Tasia. Melissa and Tasia. The lying, the cheating —

"Oh, I know her all right," I said furiously. "I

know her pretty goddamn well. You cheat! You liar! You hurt me, you're hurting her —" The words spilled.

"You and Tasia?" Melissa sputtered.

"Yeah, me and Tasia." I was hanging from a cliff, ready to plunge and not caring. "I went to her window late, sat on her fucking fence and cried like a cat until she let me in!" Out of context, the scene sounded extraordinarily ridiculous.

"She told you about *that*? She told you *that*!" A tangled look of rage and disbelief tightened her face. "Well, fuck her. Fuck you both." Melissa grabbed the fliers, dropped them in the trash and stormed out.

"Yeah, fuck us both," I muttered. I reached under the table and slipped the journal back into my briefcase.

. . . the best way to get over her is to meet someone new . . .

I retrieved a flier from the wastebasket and laid it on the table. I felt confident. I felt certain. A genie, a purveyor of fantasy, I'd take her on a magic carpet away from it all.

Staring blankly at *The Shining,* I took several slow, deep breaths. Never more alone but with nothing to lose, I waited for my Tasia and her generous reward.

CARNIVAL GIRL

seeks roller-coaster rebel for intrigue and passion. No stranger to your dark side, you are not afraid to flirt with mine. Bored with mundane merry-go-rounds, I'm looking for the fast ride, the wild ride, the make-my-heart-pound, stomach-plunge-to-the-ground ride.

Tracy Lenman's crush on Stephie McBride had started long before they were roommates. For three months, Tracy had attended a twelve-step program for love addicts. She had originally joined the group to work through her obsession with her brother's wife. Every week she participated in the meetings, but the preoccupation with her sister-in-law didn't diminish . . . that is, until the night Stephie walked in, sat down and started spinning her web.

Stephie had been abandoned by a tornado of a gal named Lee. The intensity of Stephie's desperate desire for Lee intrigued Tracy. Tracy's fixation on her sister-in-law withered in direct proportion to her interest in Stephie. Each Thursday night at the love-addicts meetings, as Stephie revealed more torrid details of her affair with Lee, Tracy rocked in a sea of what-ifs. What if she had the chance? Could she step into Lee's empty shoes? Could she carry it off? Charm Stephie the way Lee did?

And then, in an unexpected stroke of good fortune, Tracy's life took a sudden turn for the better.

"Lee's moved on," Stephie tearfully reported on that fateful Thursday night. She shook her head despondently. "She's headed to Las Vegas." There was a moment of silence and then Stephie added, "I guess it's really over." She shrugged, then glanced briefly across the room. To the far wall? To Tracy? "I've got a room for rent now, if anyone knows anyone —"

Tracy knew someone, all right. Two weeks later she was Stephie's roommate. At first, Tracy was content simply to languish in the details of Stephie's life.

"Lee was wild," Stephie confided one night after dinner. "In bedroom closets at ritzy parties, she'd push me between expensive silks and fuck me there. In dark corners of movie theaters, she'd press me

90

against cool walls and have me. I had to be so quiet.
I couldn't make a sound — once at a wedding, once at
a baby shower —"

Slippery, complex, with an on-the-edge style that
sizzled — Lee would be a hard act to follow. Tracy
tried to envision herself emulating Lee and winning
Stephie's attentions. In bed at night, fantasies of how
it could be rolled through her. She'd cruise dive
bars — just like Lee did. She'd roll dice with the
boys — just like Lee did. And then she'd come home
to fuck Stephie — just like Lee did.

Come home to fuck Stephie.

The knowledge that Stephie was down the hall —
in a silk nightgown? under a perfumed quilt? naked
and masturbating quietly? — kept Tracy awake well
into the night.

Tracy lay in bed, pried her fingers into her
sopping pussy and spun another story of how it
would be. She'd come home to fuck Stephie, no
question about that. Maybe in the kitchen. Maybe in
the closet. Maybe in the bathroom . . .

. . . On the bathroom floor, Stephie is naked.
Smooth as silk, cool as ever, Tracy kneels between
Stephie's legs. She knows how to please a woman.
More than Lee, better than Lee — not in the tub, not
on the sink, Tracy has much more creativity than
that. She dips a washcloth in the steaming tub water
and returns her attention to Stephie. Stephie spreads

her legs even farther apart. Her beefy clit juts out between mink-lined lips. Like a glittery, fat ruby, the flesh is deep red and wet. Tracy drapes the cloth on Stephie's flat belly, reaches for another, soaks it and spreads it across her rounded breasts.

Stephie moans. Her clit looks chunky and ripe. Restraining the urge to rest her mouth on the spongy flesh and simply suck, Tracy pulls back. She has other plans. A jar of Vaseline is ready and waiting up on the basin. She swirls a Q-Tip in the Vaseline and smears the greasy gel around Stephie's clitoral wedge.

"Tracy. Tracy. Tracy," Stephie mutters.

Tracy continues to tease the entire periphery of the clit-bead, without once allowing direct contact. Like she's doodling big circles, like she's lassoing a clump of pink meat, she swabs the cotton tip around and around.

Stephie starts to grind her hips in frantic circles. Tracy recognizes that Stephie's hungry for penetration and smiles. Aiming to please — better than Lee, more clever than Lee — Tracy dips another washcloth in the tub and then wrings hot water down Stephie's bulbous sex.

"Please? Please?" Stephie's voice seems far from her body.

Tracy wraps the cloth around her fingers and slowly rubs the rough towel across Stephie's engorged snatch. Up, over the clit and down to her slit. Up, over and in.

Stephie squirms. Stephie squeals.

Tracy pushes her cloth-sheathed finger past the ribbed entrance. She'd bathe Stephie. She'd cleanse Stephie. She'd wash away any trace of Lee, once and for all. Tracy fucks her with one washcloth-covered finger. She fucks her real sweet.

But there's more, so much more, she'll do for Stephie. Tracy grabs her toothbrush — on the basin, ready to go, extra soft for oral stimulation — and skims it across Stephie's square nipples, across the erect buds, over the belly and down to Stephie's clit. Back to the nipples, down to the clit, again and again until she ends the sequence by inserting the brush head right into Stephie's gaping cunt.

The clitoral sack has doubled in size and Tracy can barely contain herself. She sucks it into her mouth and pulls it, kneads it like a flabby, large teat. And in the toothbrush goes. Combing against the G-spot, scrubbing against the G-spot — in that toothbrush goes.

Stephie starts to jerk. Come squirts everywhere. Tracy draws the entire pod of clit flesh into her mouth . . .

A knock on the door slammed Tracy out of Stephie, out of the bathroom, and back into bed.

"Tracy, are you up?" Stephie's words were tinged with despair.

Tracy pulled her hand from her drenched pussy. "Stephie?" Her voice cracked. "Stephie?" She wiped her hand on the blanket and climbed out of bed.

"It's the bed," Stephie said softly through the door. "I can't sleep with it facing the door that Lee walked through. Could you, maybe, help me move it?"

God. The room smelled like pussy.

A small surge of attitude filled Tracy — after all, hadn't she just fucked Stephie pretty damn good? "Sure." She wiped her hand one last time. "I'll be right there."

Mustering all of her strength, Tracy single-handedly rearranged Stephie's bedroom furniture and then concentrated on trying to pull Stephie from her gloom. It was a difficult and grueling task. Nothing pleased Stephie for long. *Perhaps the bed should face the window?* and Tracy moved the furniture again. *Perhaps the bed should face the bathroom?* Tracy injured her back that first night and subsequently visited her chiropractor twice a week for the rest of the month ... and Stephie continued to cry every night.

The personal ad idea was originally Stephie's. Sprawled on Stephie's bed late one Friday night, they were watching "General Hospital" and stuffing themselves with a fresh supply of cheese loops.

"Thanks for making the midnight run to the store. *Again.*" Stephie gave her a hug. "You've been such a good friend these last few weeks, putting up with my moment-to-moment idiosyncrasies." Stephie shifted to a sitting position and glanced around the room. As if a switch were unexpectedly clicked, Stephie's face fell, sadness written on it. "Jesus, there's so much here that reminds me of Lee."

Oh shit, not the furniture again, Tracy silently

pleaded. She closed her eyes and waited for the telltale words — *perhaps the bed should face . . .*

"You've done so much to help me reconcile things, but I miss her. I look around the room and see her everywhere. I hate that."

Not the furniture. Not the furniture. Eyelids clenched, Tracy tried to restrain a hiss. She forced herself to relax her hands that had inadvertently tightened into rocklike fists. Slowly, with a releasing breath, she recalled her compassion for Stephie and opened her eyes. As though in a cataleptic trance, Stephie was staring at the window.

"Perhaps if the bed were facing —"

"No!" Tracy lunged for Stephie, attempting to cram a handful of loops into her mouth. "Absolutely not!"

Wrestling, laughing, they rolled back and forth on the bed, Stephie's soft body first on top of, then beneath, then once again on top of Tracy. The rose oil fragrance Stephie wore smeared into Tracy's face, her mouth, her nose. Stephie's necklace, laden with little silver stars, tinkled like tiny wind chimes.

Like a heated breeze on a hot summer night, like a midnight walk through a rose garden — Stephie was all over Tracy . . . and it was good. It was so good that Tracy deliberated going for the gold. Back on top of Stephie, holding her down, Tracy prepared to kiss Stephie, kiss her hard, kiss her like she had wanted to do since that first Thursday night.

Stephie giggled and pushed Tracy aside. She grabbed some cheese loops, threw them haphazardly at Tracy and ran for the safety of a locked bathroom door.

Alone on the bed, Tracy was enmeshed in the

spinning scent of rose oil. *If only, if only, if only.*
Tracy imagined sweet Stephie, deliciously naked, in
her arms. How long would it take Stephie to realize
that right in her home, hell, right in her bed, was a
woman, the woman, willing to do anything to make
her smile? If Stephie wanted the furniture moved
again, so be it!

"Do you want me to move the bed?" Tracy called.
"I will, you know I will, if you really want me to.
You know I'd do anything."

"Anything?" Stephie said provocatively through the
closed bathroom door.

Tracy listened intently. What did Stephie have in
mind? Was this it, that long-awaited, highly-
anticipated moment when Stephie would come to her
senses and see Tracy for the available woman she
was?

"Halle-fucking-lujah," Tracy muttered. She climbed
out of bed. "Anything, Stephie."

The toilet flushed, the bathroom door opened and
Stephie walked out. With a newspaper in her hand
and a sultry smile on her face, she said, "Would you
help me write a personal ad?"

Stephie grabbed a spiral notebook and pen and
flopped, belly flat, on the bed. Tracy toppled down
next to her. Shoulder to shoulder, amid whispers and
intimate giggles, they wrote the ad. It was
straightforward and to the point, about someone like
Lee.

As much as she hated seeing Stephie saddened,
Tracy couldn't deny the greedy pleasure Stephie's

newfound attention brought her. Every night that Stephie stayed home was a night for Tracy. Every minute that Stephie cried on Tracy's shoulder was a minute for Tracy. Who else knew the little ways to make Stephie smile or would shove a heavy nineteen-forties vanity from wall to wall without a complaint? Hungry? Taken care of. Depressed? No problem. Tracy was there and would always be.

So when Stephie walked out of that bathroom, newspaper in hand, asking for help with a personal ad, there was no question that she would comply. The asking and the nodding of the head were merely formalities.

Stephie rolled to her side and curtained her eyes with the sheet of paper. "Do you think it's too specific?"

Her movement swirled the scent of rose. Lightly at first, the summertime fragrance seemed to build upon itself. With each breath, Tracy became more and more webbed in the silky trap of desire. And the roses were as smooth as Stephie's satin skin, were as soft as Stephie's heavenly breasts. Tracy closed her eyes and thousands of petals caressed her. A floral tornado engulfed her. Erratic sparks of passion fanned into a pulsating fire. Tracy could barely speak. *This was her chance. This was her chance.* She should take Stephie in her arms. Was there any reason not to? She should kiss her on the lips. Was there any reason to wait? She should tell her all the things she'd wanted to say. Was there ever a better time?

"Too specific?" Tracy's voice always cracked at the worst times. She shifted to her side. Stephie's breasts were a mere kiss away. An electrically-charged boundary seemed to surround Stephie. Tracy couldn't see it, but knew all too well it was there. Rejection was not pretty. If she handled this poorly, if she offended Stephie, she'd be on her ass, fried to a crisp, in a matter of seconds. There had to be some way to wake her up, to make her realize that her fast ride, her wild ride, her roller-coaster rebel was already here. "It's specific but then, let's not forget, you're not very flexible."

Stephie turned toward Tracy and put the ad down. They were close, so close, that their lips could have touched if one, or the other, were to move a scant inch or two more.

"This could be a new beginning for me." Stephie seemed lost in a dream.

Tracy regarded her carefully. Stephie had a certain vitality, a drawing power, that was unlike any woman Tracy knew. Attractive in a low-key androgynous way, Stephie called herself femme, insisted she was femme and often wore dangling necklaces and earrings to make her point.

Stephie was a borderline femme who was caught in the illusion of wanting a tough-ass butch. So maybe Tracy's body was a bit on the soft side, was that so bad? She could move a dresser along with the best. If she worked with it — the right gel, weather conditions providing — her short, baby-fine hair would probably slick back — at least temporarily. She could be everything Lee was, given the chance. Stephie's lips were a scant inch away . . .

It was moments like this, lying next to Stephie, so near that they were almost kissing — or had they, on another level, already kissed? — that Tracy wondered how to cross that line without suffering electrocution.

Tracy thought hard and finally said, "You can use

my P.O. box number. Hell, I go there every day. That way you don't have the weekly delay of waiting for the paper to send the replies."

"Great idea!" Stephie popped up. "Oh, Tracy, what would I ever do without you?"

Still absorbed in thought, Tracy just smiled.

Even though it was more than convenient for Stephie to pick up the mail, even though Tracy had to make an out-of-the-way trip to check the box, Tracy refused to surrender the key. For her plan to unfold smoothly, it was essential that she maintain control of the mail.

"Let me be in on some of the fun," Tracy had insisted. "You're the letter-opener and I'm the retriever."

Stephie protested, but no matter what she said or how she pleaded, Tracy had the key and Tracy got the mail.

"Anything today?" Stephie would ask the moment Tracy walked in.

"Nah, not today," Tracy would reply nonchalantly.

Day after day, Tracy came through the door and tossed the mail, *her* mail, onto the kitchen table. *Nah, none today,* she'd say with a shrug. And although replies did arrive, Tracy had tossed them into the trash can before leaving the post office. After all, there was only one letter that Stephie would ever see, and it hadn't arrived yet.

More and more on edge, Stephie wanted the living room couch moved into her bedroom and the vanity out — just to give herself a new perspective — but Tracy urged her to be patient.

"It's only been a week," Tracy said calmly, flopping Friday's mail onto the table. Pleased with herself, impressed that she had played her hand so well, Tracy crossed the kitchen with a strut so cocky that for a moment, she believed herself to be as butch as Lee. "You've got to give this kind of thing time."

"Easy for you to say." Stephie followed her to the cupboard and appraised the empty shelf. "Imagine terribly wanting something and not being able to have it."

"Listen, Steph," Tracy softened her voice. "Things are going to look up. I just know it."

The next day, having plastered on her best I-told-you-so smile, Tracy opened the front door and waved a letter. "Look here. Look here! Postmarked San Francisco. A city girl? A high roller? What do you think?" In a small circle, the letter raised above her head, she did a mock jig. Stephie leapt for the mail, and with a grandiose bow, Tracy presented it to her. "Your majesty?"

"Tracy, Tracy, Tracy!" Stephie cried. She grabbed the envelope and ripped it open. "Oh, my God, listen to this! Listen to this!"

As if the contents would be a surprise, as if she had no idea what was written on that note, Tracy leaned against the couch and waited to hear Stephie read each fastidiously chosen word, each precisely structured thought.

" 'My dear carnival girl.' " Stephie brought the letter to her breasts and whirled in a circle. "She called me 'carnival girl.' "

A breeze of giddy amusement bounced from the walls then skipped around the room. Tracy coasted on the gust of joy as the words swirled. *My dear carnival girl. My dear, dear carnival girl.*

" 'Since you and I are both looking for the fast ride, the wild ride —' " Stephie's breath was short as she frolicked through the words. " '— I'll make your heart pound, your stomach plunge to the ground —' "

Tracy stopped listening. Having labored with a thesaurus until four in the morning the week before, having taken a day off work to drive forty-five miles for a San Francisco postmark, she knew all too well what that letter said. Incredibly clever, she thought, but foolproof? She certainly hoped so. Stephie had asked for a wild ride, a fast ride. Let someone else move the couch to the bedroom. From this moment on, she, Tracy Lenman, was buying tickets for the roller coaster.

An unwonted flush animated Stephie's face. There was absolutely no question that she was intrigued, excited, thrilled. Exhilaration electrified the room. Tracy could almost feel the rumble of the carnival ride, the climbing of that first peak.

"Listen to this!" Stephie rushed to Tracy's side. With trembling fingers, she pointed at the sentence. " 'Our amusement park will be the Women's Weekend at Russian River. I'm willing to come north to find you. I'm willing to do what it takes. I'll be at Ziggurat Dance Club on Saturday night, waiting for you. Are you willing to do what it takes?' " Stephie made a fist, inadvertently crumpling the letter. "Am I willing? Am I willing?" She gave Tracy a mock push and laughed. "This woman has no idea how willing I am!"

Yeah, right, Tracy thought. She fought the abrupt, insane urge to grab the letter and smooth that wrinkled page she'd worked on all night.

As if subconsciously following Tracy's will, Stephie flattened the letter and continued reading. " 'I'll be at the club for a single hour. If you find me, then prepare for the ride of your life. One chance and one chance only. A flower in my lapel is how you'll know.' "

Like tiny red lights, the words spun in the darkness of Tracy's closed eyes. Oh yes, Tracy had a roller-coaster ride for Stephie. Something to lift her off her feet and reel her through space. A ride she'd never forget.

Stephie hung up the phone and added another name to the list. "There will be hundreds of women at Ziggurat." She dropped the notepad on the table. "But I've got no intention of letting her slip past me."

"Don't you think you're going a little overboard with this thing?" Tracy tried to veil her irritation. "How many of our friends are you going to drag into this thing?" She grabbed the list of names and shot Stephie a look of contempt. "Jesus, if this mystery woman gets wind that there's a twenty-five-dollar bounty on her, she's going to walk and never look back."

"*A,* she'll never find out," Stephie said firmly. "And *B,* it's all in good fun."

"Why did you recruit everyone we know?" Tracy scanned the names.

"Why's it such a big deal to you how I do it?"

"I just hate to see you invest so much in someone you know nothing about," Tracy said defensively. "All you've done since you got the damned letter is talk on the phone or sit in your room and fantasize. We hardly spend any time together anymore." She tossed the notepad back on the table. "What if this woman's a clown? What if she's a phony? Hell, what if she doesn't show? Won't you be embarrassed that you've got twenty friends searching for her? And if she is there, how will it be having everyone watch every goddamn move we make?"

"*We?*" Stephie said sharply. "Look, if it's too much for you, don't get involved." She grabbed the list and stormed out of the room.

"Don't worry, I won't," Tracy called after her.

The room was suddenly empty. Tracy dragged from the table to the couch. "Oh God, oh God," she mumbled. Her head began to pound. All of their friends' names were on that list. Tracy had a fleeting vision of the entire gang combing Ziggurat in search of the flower-lapeled woman.

Well, too bad for everyone, because *that* woman was going be a no-show, Tracy thought sourly. There was no way in hell she'd go through with her scheme now, not with a brigade of women keeping vigilance. Her marvelous plan to impress Stephie with a clever approach, a cunning technique, a dazzling finale, was fizzling as grim reality set in. Roller-coaster hot-shot to laughingstock fool was a very ugly descent.

"It was *you* who sent the letter?" The circle of friends would laugh.

"*You* think of yourself as a roller-coaster rebel?" They would howl.

"*You're* going to make Stephie's heart pound, her stomach plunge?" They'd roll on the floor.

Had Stephie kept her mouth shut, allowing Tracy to subtly make her moves, then yes, Tracy could have displayed her talents in a brilliant tour de force. Her idea to use her P.O. box, to destroy the other letters that came for Stephie, was a stroke of genius. Was that not dark enough, daring enough to catch any woman's eye? And now her strategy had gone askew, compromised by Stephie's inability to keep personal matters private.

Disappointed and slightly nauseous, Tracy headed toward the bedroom. Her reflection in the hall mirror — limp hair, round face, short stature — stared despondently back. Some roller-coaster rebel.

Well past midnight, Tracy left the confines of her room for a snack. A blue light flickered at the end of the hall. Intuitively, Tracy slowed. From the dark, she peeked into the living room. A porno movie flashed on the TV screen. Stephie was on the couch, an afghan bunched across her thighs. Her arm was partially hidden beneath the coverlet, but Tracy could see the intensity with which it beat back and forth. Her own arm twitched in jealous commiseration.

Arched back, body stiff with hard-earned pleasure, Stephie strummed herself. Desperately aroused, Tracy could hardly keep from racing back to her bed. With the pussy-watering image of Stephie fresh in her mind, Tracy knew she'd climax in a flash.

It was a sleazy urge and Tracy knew it. To exploit the sight she had inadvertently stumbled upon for her own perverse desire was despicable. As difficult as it was, Tracy's extreme loyalty to Stephie triumphed over her unsavory impulse to dash off to bed. So stiff that her back would ache in the morning, Tracy held her ground.

Was the air really saturated with Stephie's sea-musk scent? Could Tracy actually hear the flapping sound each time Stephie's fingers slapped the oily flesh? Tracy peeked around the corner. Stephie was wilder than Tracy could have imagined. Nonstop, Stephie continued her furious pace. Without a break, she pounded her pussy. Faster, harder, more and more.

Tracy pressed hard against the wall. Perhaps she should go back to her room? Her heart thumped, her mouth was dry. Perhaps she should . . . ? She dipped her hand into her sweatpants. Her pussy was sloppy-wet.

"Oh God, oh, oh yes, yes, okay, yes —" An onrush of Stephie's whispered words ricocheted down the hallway and faded into sudden silence. Alarmed, Tracy shot to her room and quickly closed the door. She leaned against the door. Her breathing was hard, fast, intense. She should have never watched. She should have never, ever watched.

A victim of circumstance and an honorable friend, Tracy felt an immediate obligation to erase the incident from her mind. She absolutely would not lie in her bed, she would not put her fingers back on her clit and she definitely would not think of Stephie.

But that sticky vision — Stephie with her legs wide, her hand pumping her pussy at high rpm's — slithered from the floor, up Tracy's legs in a slow, hot wave of intoxicating lust.

As if she could somehow coax the image to ooze out, Tracy dashed across the room and popped the window open. But the air was thin, leaving her gasping in the overwhelming, damp scent of Stephie's sea-musk pussy.

Tightened to a thick, bunched knot, Tracy's clitoris ached hard. She stumbled to the bed. Between her mattresses was the double-ended dildo. *Oh yeah, oh yeah, oh yeah, oh yeah.* She yanked down her pants, she grabbed the dildo. *Oh yeah, oh yeah, oh yeah, oh yeah.* Into her drenched, swollen cunt, she smeared her fingers and scooped her creamy dew over the dildo heads.

She nudged one bulbous head against her greedy slit and with a quick thrust, popped it in. She didn't want to exploit, knew she that shouldn't — but she just couldn't get the luscious picture of Stephie out of her mind.

It was Stephie on the couch, arched and hot. It was Stephie with the afghan haphazardly covering her thighs. Stephie, with her arm going and going. Was Stephie's pussy soaked as she rubbed it down? Was it bulbous? Was it hard? Was it pink? Was it rippled?

Tracy curved the long dildo and teased the other end against the puckered portal of her ass. *Oh yeah, oh yeah, oh yeah.* It was good. So good. She inched the second tip into the tiny crack, slow, slow, then drove it in with one quick jerk. Uncomfortably sweet. Deliciously tight. She let out a long, low gasp. Her pussy clamped tight. In and out. In and out. Her ass sucked the thick intruder. In and out. In and out — her cunt, her ass, her cunt. Had Stephie been arched as high as Tracy was now? As tight? As wet? As wild? *Oh yeah, baby. Oh yeah, yeah, yeah.*

There was little doubt about Stephie's frame of mind Saturday morning. Tracy was awakened by Stephie's knock on the bedroom door. With a cheerful hum, Stephie laid a breakfast tray — including morning paper and crystal-vased rosebud — on Tracy's lap.

"Sorry I've been so self-absorbed lately," Stephie said with an apologetic smile. "It's just that organizing things for tonight has taken so much —"

"I know, I understand," Tracy interrupted. She was in no mood to hear, once again, Stephie's big plans for the night. She crunched on a slice of bacon, savoring its perfectly crisp texture. It was cooked exactly the way she liked it. God, Stephie could be so damn caring when she wanted to be.

On the edge of the bed, Stephie chattered incessantly about the upcoming evening's espionage. Her words fluttered around her in a flurry of excitement. "You'll be at my side, won't you? I can't imagine not having you there." Stephie's tone was insistent.

"Of course I'll be with you," Tracy said sweetly. "How could I desert you now?" Tracy munched another piece of bacon and reconsidered the turn of events. Oh, she'd go with Stephie to Ziggurat, all right. How unfortunate when the woman with the flower didn't make an appearance. How disappointing. What a considerable let-down.

Stephie would fall into depression, Tracy knew that. The bed would have to be moved — maybe twice in one night. But Tracy would be there, like she always was, to soothe poor Stephie and to help pick up the shattered pieces. She'd take care of Stephie — hold her, listen to her, soothe her. Somewhere in those moments of tenderness, when the slippery boundaries between friends become indistinct and blurred, Tracy would offer Stephie the ride of her life.

"It's almost midnight." Stephie scanned the smoke-filled club again. "Do you think we missed her in the crowd?"

Tracy stared through the stream of women and then glanced at Stephie. Her lips pursed, her focus darting desperately around the room, Stephie moved closer and lightly rested her hand on Tracy's arm. Tracy glanced at her watch. Rebel girl was a no-show and, as far as she was concerned, it was time to leave.

"Oh my God." Stephie's fingers dug into Tracy's arm. "Oh, my God. Oh, my God. There she is. There she is!"

Stephie was halfway across the room before Tracy pinpointed the dark-haired woman, standing in the corner — a goddamned flower on her white, collared shirt. Leather chaps accentuated the woman's strong build. She was smiling like a predator at dawn.

Tracy stood immobilized as Stephie pushed through the shadows. The woman seemed nonchalant, cool, unsuspecting as Stephie approached.

"So I said, 'Are you my fast ride, my wild ride?' " The words seemed to spark around Stephie in tiny fireworks. Her eyes sparkled. Her entire face radiated excitement. "And she says, I swear to God, she says it just like this —" Stephie lowered her voice and cocked her head back with attitude. " 'Your wild ride?' And then, listen to this, just listen to this! — she looks me up and down, real seductively and says, 'You got a ticket?' "

" 'You got a ticket?' That's what she said?" Misery cracked Tracy's voice.

"Then she hands me this blindfold —" Stephie waved a scarf in Tracy's face. "— and tells me to sit in the red corvette parked right out front, put on the blindfold and wait ten minutes."

Tracy tried to think fast. There had to be a way to slow things down, to get a grip on the situation before she lost Stephie once and for all. "Sounds risky to me," was the best she could come up with on such short notice.

"I'll be back." Stephie turned away. "My wild ride's ready to start."

* * * * *

Three minutes. Five minutes. The roller-coaster woman was still in the corner when Tracy left the club. Stephie was in the front seat of the corvette. The scarf was tied around her eyes.

Without a word, Tracy opened the passenger side, took Stephie by the hand and led her into the trees.

"You want a wild ride? A fast ride?" Tracy's hard, low tone sounded foreign, even to herself.

"Yes, yes," Stephie pleaded as she stepped haphazardly, clinging tightly to Tracy's arm.

Tracy escorted her to a large, flat stump. "Want the dark side, baby? I'll give you the dark side." Stephie's skirt hiked to her creamy thighs as she was guided, face down, over the stump.

"Dark. Wild." Stephie murmured.

Tracy raised Stephie's skirt up, revealing her ample, heart-shaped ass.

"No panties?" Tracy muttered. "No fucking panties."

Without thought, Tracy dipped a finger into Stephie's wet sex. One finger — and she fucked her, fucked her good. A second finger slipped in. She burrowed. She plunged. She was buying a ticket. She was leading Stephie to the Ferris wheel. Up and up and up they'd go.

As if a bolt of lightning hit her, Tracy suddenly blazed with butch bravado. She was cool. She was smooth. Another finger. Another. Her hair wasn't slicked, didn't matter — she was hell on wheels. Her biceps weren't hard, didn't matter, she could fuck Stephie for the rest of the night. And on and on — all of her fingers had disappeared somewhere between Stephie's fleshy cheeks. It was damp, dark, like a roller-coaster ride into soft sweet pussy.

Stephie was rocking and moving and seemed out of her mind with pleasure. Tracy had no idea how all her fingers had slid so easily into Stephie. Didn't matter. Tracy was tough. She was smooth. She was fire.

Tracy swirled her fist in the secret juices. Stephie's open cunt sucked and sucked. Tracy didn't stop, wouldn't stop. She could go all night. Stephie whimpered and moaned as her body shuddered in ongoing spasms. Covered with sweat and sex, Stephie finally collapsed onto the stump.

Now what? Now the hell what? Tracy peered back through the trees toward the parking lot as she eased her fist from Stephie's pulsating cunt. She could run and not look back, be in the club — cool, nonchalant — when Stephie returned.

Stephie began to untie the scarf.

Time was running out. It was now or never. With all the butch attitude she had, Tracy whispered, "No stranger to your dark side, you are not afraid to flirt with mine . . ."

"Carnival Girl . . ." The scarf fell from Stephie's eyes as she turned to face her future.

An impulsive glance into Charlotte's mirror triggered my graceless descent into a lousy mood. Originally, I had gone into her bathroom to pee. Somehow, without forethought of any kind, I found myself balanced precariously on the sink, engrossed in a depressing evaluation of my thighs. Because the mirror in that bathroom is four feet from the floor, because I had no desire to explain what I was doing perched on her sink, I decided not to mention the incident to Charlotte. Consequently, I was stuck in that living hell of not knowing whether Charlotte's bathroom mirror was what we considered a good mirror.

A good mirror was user friendly — like the one in the third dressing room to the left, in Macy's second-floor, Anne Klein department. In that mirror, we were always tall and slim. No matter where I was in that store, when it came time to try something on, it was to the second floor, third stall to the left that I headed. Charlotte bought pants at the Gap, carried them to Macy's and tried them on there. To feel less bloated during her last PMS, Terri had sex with Sandy in that very stall. It's standard procedure — when any of us discovers a good mirror, we spread the word.

We had an unwritten agreement not to react to a reflection until we had available data on the mirror's nature. Knowing all that, I had pulled down my jeans and climbed on Charlotte's sink anyway. In an unsteady squat, I straddled the border of the basin like a monster toad. I pivoted until I faced away from the mirror and then, throwing all caution to the wind, I peered over my shoulder at my butt and thighs — my fleshy, larger-than-I-had-remembered butt and thighs.

Was this a good mirror reflecting a bad prognosis or simply a bad mirror? There was only one way to be certain. The full-length on Charlotte's closet was a good mirror. Depressed? Stand in front of Charlotte's closet mirror. Ate too much? Charlotte's mirror was the place to be. With pants bunched around one ankle, I climbed down from the sink and headed to the bedroom where the good mirror offered better odds.

"What's up?" Sprawled across her bed, Charlotte looked up from the newspaper she was reading.

"I feel fat," I muttered, peering at my Jockeys-for-Her-covered butt in the mirror.

"Mirror in the bathroom is bad," she offered offhandedly. "*I* stay off that sink unless I'm looking to feel bad."

I shot her a smirk then focused on my thighs. Even in the good mirror, they seemed flabby. "Something wrong with this mirror, too?" It was an overcast day, maybe the lighting was bad.

Charlotte shrugged and returned her attention to the paper.

"Maybe I need to stop eating." I was sliding into a funk. "God, wasn't I thinner when I first got here?" Heading full throttle into bleakness, I bent over and attempted another perspective of my rear end.

Charlotte whistled. "You look good to me."

"I'm fat." I slumped to the floor. "And it's only going to get worse. I hate diets. I hate gyms . . . Do I look bigger to you?"

"Come here and bend over so I can check," Charlotte said with a seductive edge in her voice.

"I'm serious." I was headed into that dreaded, dark, body-image pit. My destiny was already mapped out — unless I got to a better mirror, I was going to be miserable.

"Jennifer, you look fine."

"Hah!" Gloomy and resistant to compliments, I pouted in the corner.

"Well..." Charlotte hesitated, most probably looking for a way to lasso me out of the muck. "We could do some aerobics. A half-hour with Jane Fonda and I promise you'll feel better."

"I'd need more than a half-hour with Jane," I said quickly. "And believe me, it wouldn't be aerobics that I'd want to do with her. Know what I mean?" I stood up, tugged my pants to my waist and reluctantly reassessed my butt. I had to admit, once snugly packed in the jeans, my ass did look better. Obviously, the secret to a good mirror was to be dressed. I checked my profile from each side. "Anyway, I hate aerobics."

"Here's something. Look at this." Charlotte angled the newspaper toward me. "We could hire a personal trainer. Now there's a great idea."

I flopped on the bed next to Charlotte and scanned the ad. " 'Satisfaction guaranteed'? That brings me back to the question of Ms. Fonda..."

Charlotte grabbed the paper and gave me a swat. "Really, what do you think?"

One last glimpse in the mirror afforded me a reprieve from what could have been an ugly, all-day snit. From a distance, on the bed, I appeared thinner. Why exercise when I could look just as good lying down? "Nah." I pulled the paper from Charlotte and searched for the comics. "I'm feeling better now."

I felt relatively fit the rest of the afternoon but

when I got home, a compulsive urge to climb on my own sink for one final appraisal consumed me. After all, my sink mirror was a good one. Didn't my face always look young in that mirror? More provocative? Less harsh?

The bathroom sink was not perch-friendly. Prodded by an insistent desire for truth, nonetheless, I managed to prop myself on the basin in an unstable squat. One dreadful minute later, I was off that sink, away from the ruthless mirror, and desperately searching the classifieds for that personal ad.

Her name was Renn Harding, although when I first walked through the door of her gym — a converted out-building behind her house — and saw her carrying a weight-laden barbell across the room, the only portion of her name that came to mind was the Hard. Dressed in a pair of spandex shorts and a tank top, she was rock-solid. Her tanned shoulders and arms were beautifully sculpted. Her biceps were distinct, her triceps tight. Each muscle — each strong, smooth muscle — made its presence known with every movement she made.

"Hello, Jennifer." She offered a friendly smile and a persuasive handshake. Had I stepped into *Muscle and Fitness* and clasped hands with Ms. Olympia, I doubt I would have been more impressed.

I stood there, my small hand smothered in hers, and all I could think of, all I wanted to say was, *hard. Hard. Hard. Hard.* Had I said spoken yet? Had I said hello? *Hello, Ms. Hard?* I felt lightheaded and entranced. "Hello Ms. Hard —"

"Please, call me Renn," she interrupted. "No need for formalities."

"Of course." I smiled. My gaze slid from her steady eyes to her magnificent arms and finally centered on her well-shaped hands. "Renn."

I fought a wild impulse to grasp her hand even tighter and force it into my gym shorts, but Renn loosened her grip and stepped back. She just stood there, staring intently into my eyes.

"So you want to firm up," she said, without asking.

And what could I say? In that moment, various parts of me already felt extremely firm. "Yes. Firm."

Renn regarded me carefully. Her eyes focused on my shoulders then seductively drifted to my breasts. A simple glance, yet her eyes felt like desperate fingers. White heat tightened my nipples. Sensations rumbled through me — as if her lips had already surrounded the erect flesh, had sucked it, had rolled it. Across my belly, to my sex-scented hair, I imagined her tongue stirring up a storm of desire.

"You're in pretty good shape." Renn's attention returned to my eyes. "We'll start with light weights and plenty of reps. Let's warm up." She crossed to the mirror-covered wall and gestured for me to join her.

Let's warm up? She bent over and touched her toes. Her firm back V-ed to a trim waist and hips. Her ass curved strong — I was warming up, all right. Like a sleek jungle cat, her legs were well-muscled and firm — I felt limber, pliable and ready to go. Her midnight-hued hair, cut short and slicked back, accentuated her squinty, dark-fringed eyes. She looked tough, yet cool. Light-years beyond warm, eons

117

beyond warm, I was ready to bench press whatever she offered.

She was exciting. She was incredible. I watched her reflection in the mirror. She smiled then reached high with her arms. She was "warming up." I was getting hot. That burning, age-old question immediately came to mind — was she a lesbian? She had a butch attitude, a butch stance — but was she a lesbian? Had her knee-knocking appraisal earlier merely been that of an enthusiastic trainer evaluating her client or was it a more-than-interested butch sizing up a femme? Eager to find out, I approached her.

I hate the precarious nature of wrong assumptions. Charlotte, who last year had appointed herself as my social mentor, had tried to convince me that lesbians had a special radar for each other.

"You just have to look a woman in the eyes," Charlotte had said. "If she's a dyke, you'll know it."

I recalled my first and last test of Charlotte's theory. The local grocery store cashier — the one that Charlotte had bet me twenty dollars was a dyke — had seemed very friendly each time I went in. I suspected she was a lesbian — her short spiked hair, her flirty smile — and brought Charlotte in for her expert opinion. Charlotte pestered me the whole way home. "Of course she's a dyke." Charlotte blew a large pink gum bubble and popped it. "She wants you, Jennifer. Hell, she told you her break was in fifteen minutes and that she smokes by the phone booth. Do you think that was just small talk? She wants you to show up — she was making her move. Let's go for it!"

Only out as a lesbian for a few months and

dependent on Charlotte's years of vast experience, I let her convince me to turn back. Somewhere between the U-turn and pulling into the parking lot, "Let's go for it" had metamorphosed into "You go for it. I'll wait in the car."

"You mean, do this alone?" I stammered as I clicked off the ignition.

"I can't be there. It will ruin the entire mystique of your approach."

As much as I didn't like Charlotte's theory, it did seem to make sense. "So what do I say?" I said half-heartedly.

"Ask her to dinner. I guarantee, she'll pick it up from there."

"And what if she's not a lesbian." I cringed at the possible consequences of unintentionally approaching an uptight straight woman.

"Okay then —" Charlotte blew another bubble and popped it with her finger. "Just ask her if she dates women, that ought to settle things."

"Just walk up to her and ask if she dates women? Are you crazy?" I collapsed into doubt.

"She's a dyke, for God's sake. This is my area of expertise. I've got twenty bucks that says she is." Charlotte pulled a twenty from her coat pocket and waggled it in front of my face. "Now, go ask her to dinner."

Charlotte never waved cash unless she was certain. I took a slow breath, slapped five with Charlotte and headed toward the phone booth. From a few cars away, I spotted the cashier leaning against the building. I called on my lesbian radar for one last once-over.

She wore army boots — *and is probably a dyke,*

the radar hummed. With attitude, she tossed the cigarette to the pavement, crossed the parking lot and unlocked a Toyota truck — *and is probably a dyke,* the radar replied. Back toward the store, with a butch strut — *probably a dyke.*

"Hey," I called. *She wants you to show up, she was making her move* — Charlotte's words egged me on.

She turned to face me. "Oh hi." She smiled. "Forget something?"

Yeah, you, I thought, nervous and cocky all at once. "Can I ask you a question?" We'd go to dinner. I'd play femme and relatively hard to get but in the end, we'd go to her place and have sex on her couch.

"Sure." She walked over to me. As if uncertain of what I wanted, she appraised me curiously. The queasy feeling that Charlotte might be way off-base suddenly washed over me. Did I say, "How about dinner?" And what if Charlotte was wrong? Did I ask if she dated women? And what if Charlotte was wrong? My tongue felt frozen. My heart pounded in my chest.

"What's up?" she asked.

"Do you date women?" I muttered, pushing the words out as quickly as possible.

"Excuse me?" The cashier stepped closer.

I wanted to turn and run but it was too late. She was inches away — staring, wondering, waiting. "Do you date women?" I repeated like a cornered Kinsey reporter.

"Is this some kind of a weird joke?" The butch, truck-driving, Charlotte-was-certain-she-was-a-lesbian cashier did a fast one-eighty turn and raced into the grocery. She didn't look back.

Charlotte had said she was sorry, had admitted that these situations were rare but unfortunately *did* happen, and had given me the twenty.

I stood next to butch-looking Renn, glared at my reflection and said nothing. She was still stretching. Her thighs bulged beneath the shiny blue spandex shorts. Her calves were full and rounded. I imagined her strength. If she wanted to, she could lift me with one arm, she could slam me against the wall, she could fuck me hard.

"Let's get you warmed up." Renn moved behind me, put her hands on my waist, and guided me into an upper torso bend. My ass pressed against her belly.

"Good, lean forward, let go." Her tone was sugary and wet. Her grip was strong.

Ass pushed against her, close to her, into her, I stretched my arms ahead.

"That's right, just like that," she coaxed. "Reach out, just let go."

My legs felt rubbery. Passion seeped from where her hands held me and pooled like thick, heated syrup between my legs. I imagined a dildo strapped around her waist. And oh, how she'd fuck me, oh how she'd drive me! I'd lean over and spread. I'd let go and let go and —

"Can you touch your toes?" Had Renn whispered or was her voice merely shadowy and low?

I wanted to press my face against that mirror while she fucked me hard with her swollen, thick rod. I'd touch my toes, I'd raise my ass. I'd do anything she asked.

"Very good." Renn's hands slid from my waist to my hips. "Very, very good."

121

And I was good, wasn't I? Bent over, just as she'd asked, touching my toes, just as she'd asked — I was very, very good. But I could be even better, if she'd just give me a chance. I could be so much better.

Renn pulled my ass tighter against her abdomen. "Now, spread your legs and reach farther ahead." I stretched forward. "Now, your toes." I touched my toes. "That's right, keep it going, move in rhythm, let it go. Forward and down. Forward and down."

I felt like the ocean, rushing in waves to a sun-baked beach. In and out. In and out. I rolled in, I flowed out. Over and over, my ass churned against her. And suddenly, as if I had never stood in front of that grocery cashier, as if I had never been humiliated beyond belief, as if I had a lesbian radar that could do me no wrong, I heard those unexpected words fly from my lips: "Renn, do you date women?"

"Excuse me?" Renn's grip on my hips seemed suddenly tenuous. Images of the offended butch cashier — pivoting in a harsh turn and hurrying into the store — flashed before me. Under Renn's supervision, dependent on her grip, I was outstretched, leaning forward and letting go. *Do you date women?* I was four meager words away from slamming headfirst to the floor.

Obviously, Renn hadn't clearly heard me. I had a chance to reword my question and prevent another embarrassing situation. My mind raced. *Do you bait women? Hate women? Rate women?* "Do you rate women, according to their progress?" I said quickly.

Renn's grip tightened on my hips and she pulled my ass even closer against her belly. "I don't think that's what you said." Her voice simmered.

"You don't?" I said meekly. I glanced in the

mirror. Renn was looking intently at me. A sly smile played on her lips and her bad-girl eyes shifted.

She shook her head then leaned down close to me. "No, I don't," she whispered in my ear. Her breath was hot. Her tone was sultry. She slid her hands up from my hips and wrapped her arms completely around my waist. If she hadn't been holding me, I was certain I would have melted into a pool of molten lava at her feet.

"What I meant was . . . I was just curious if . . ." I was pinned to her body — her hard, strong body. Her arms secured me, enclosed me, engulfed me. " . . . if you . . ." The words seemed lodged in my throat.

"If I was attracted to you? Is that what you were curious about, Jennifer?"

"Well, yes, I suppose, bottom line, that . . ."

"That I am." Renn guided me up and turned me toward her. Her hands grasped my wrists. "I think you're plenty warmed up, don't you?"

Her lips were inches from mine, seconds from mine, a heartbeat from mine. I nodded. I smiled. I prepared for her kiss.

"Prolonging the warm-up makes a session more effective, know what I mean?" Renn winked, then let go of my arms. Throbbing with desire, I stood, unable to do anything but stare as Renn approached a large Everlast boxing bag that hung from the ceiling and gave it a swift shove. "I like direct contact." Her eyes seared. Her words flared. "To challenge, to confront, to jab."

Boxing gloves hung from a hook on the wall. Renn tossed me a pair then put on a pair herself. She clenched the lace between her teeth and managed to tie the glove with her mouth. I considered her full lips, her white teeth. Did she suck hard during sex? I imagined purple welts on my breasts. Did she bite? I'd bend over in front of the mirror. Her teeth would pinch the flesh of my shoulder. She'd nip, she'd bruise. From behind, she'd poke the strapped-on dildo against my sopping slit. I'd be so creamy, I'd be so gooey. I'd press my hands against the glass and tempt her to give me all she's got. And she certainly did have it.

One-two. One-two. She punched and counter-punched. Her thighs were steel. She could probably raise me in the air and sink me up and down on her fat, thick spear without blinking an eye. Or ... or ... what if she leaned me over one of the workout benches. Leaned me right over a bench and fucked me in the ass?

I'd never done it that way — in the ass — but something about Renn brought that image to mind. I'd spread my legs nice and wide. Charlotte told me about this, how it's done. Renn would squirt cold lube down my ass slit. She'd hold my cheeks apart — or if I wanted, I could separate them for her. Yes, that's exactly what I'd do! It would be scary, it might hurt, but I wanted Renn to be the one. To challenge, to confront, to jab — she just had that quality about her.

Renn gave the bag a quick pop with her right, then with her left. Gloves untied on my hands, I leaned against the cool mirror and watched her. She was simultaneously rough and graceful. Like a dancer she stepped rhythmically, like a fighter she bobbed and ducked. Each move drew me in. She pummeled the oblong bag. Her biceps seemed thicker, bulkier.

Muscles protruded prominently beneath her spandex shorts.

In, she shuffled. Back, she jumped. She pounded, she knocked, she dipped and she swayed. Intrigued, I moved closer. Aroused, I stepped toward her. Sweat beaded on her forehead, her lip, and trickled down her neck. She made huffing sounds each time she pursued, each time she attacked. Down she swooped, up she slammed, and one-two, one-two. Boom. Boom. Boom. Boom.

I could hear her fucking me — gasping, heaving — forcing that dildo into the very place it didn't belong. "Oh please, no," I'd groan. "Oh please, yes," I'd moan. Charlotte says it pinches, but that it's good, good, good. "The secret is to relax," she had said. "Relax and take as much as you can."

The scent of Renn's perspiration swirled in tiny gusts of air. Each time she struck, my body involuntarily jerked, as if I were bent over, taking her thrusts. One-two. One-two. She was wet. She was soaked. She was fast. She was relentless.

"What do ya think?" She panted. One-two. One-two. "Wanna give it a try?"

Yes, I very much wanted to give it a try. Yes. Yes. Yes. Did she have lube? Did she have a dildo?

Renn tugged her gloves off and stepped in front of me. I wanted her to grab me, to hold me close, to smear her sweat all over me. We'd rip off our clothes and capsize to the floor and she'd slide her slippery, wet breasts across mine. We'd squish together, soft against firm. She'd glide on my body, slither on my body, slosh, slip, move effortlessly on my body. Her nipples would pop like scarlet kernels. Her pussy would rub up and down on my thigh. Slick, oily lips would leave a sex trail up my leg.

"Well, Jennifer?" Renn's words bounced between her labored breaths. "Huh, Jennifer?"

"I haven't tied my laces," I said faintly, raising my gloved hands between us.

"That's easy enough." Renn secured the laces. "You're tied. Anything else I can help you with?"

I did a quick run-through of all the subtle one-liners Charlotte had drilled into me over the year — how to imply that you want to get fucked, how to hint that you want it that very second yet still maintain some semblance of glamour.

"I want to get fucked," I blurted, immediately, undeniably and sickeningly aware that this was *not* one of the suggestions Charlotte had proposed. At this point, I was uncertain if I should simply say thanks for the workout and leave, just stare at the floor or cleverly interchange my words and repeat the statement — *I want to get ducked? lucked? trucked.*

"You want to get fucked?" Renn said in a slow, sexy tone. Her gaze seemed to pierce mine. A bolt of electricity jumped between us. Somehow, it seemed to make more sense when she said it.

"Yes, fucked." I was simply mimicking her now.

"Like in, dinner-and-then-to-my-couch kind of fuck?" She stepped in closer.

I shook my head. That once-interesting idea no longer intrigued me.

"Like, call-me-sometime kind of fuck?" The sweet mix of cologne and sweat surrounded me.

I shook my head.

"Or perhaps like, fuck me in the gym, right now, that kind of fuck."

Besides being buffed, she was also smart. I liked that in a woman. I nodded coyly.

"Do you want me to take you like I took the boxing bag?" Renn ran her finger along my jawline and down my neck. "Like that? Hard and fast and without a thought?" Her finger slid to the curve of my breasts. "You liked that, didn't you — watching me go nonstop, watching the bag just take it?"

Now that *she'd* mentioned it, I liked the idea even more than before.

With her teeth, Renn slowly pulled the tied laces of my gloves. The strings untangled and the bows gave way. She'd take off my gloves, she'd take me to that mirror. My hands on the cool glass, my ass at her disposal — I wanted to let go, give it up, once and for all.

Not removing my gloves, Renn led me to a weight machine and then, to my agreeable surprise, tied the laces to an overhead bar. My hands were bound, my arms were raised — sure, I could have pulled my hands right out of those gloves and stomped out the door — but I didn't and wouldn't and we both knew that.

Renn walked over to a gym bag, pulled out a dildo already in its harness and returned to me. As if we had done this a million times before, she pulled down my shorts.

"Nice," was all she said.

Without undressing, she stepped into the harness, belted it around her waist and gave me a grin. "Still warmed up?" Beneath my T-shirt, my nipples rippled into thick points. Their insistent outline must have caught Renn's attention because she suddenly pushed her hands beneath my shirt and squeezed both awakened tips at once. I let out an involuntary moan.

"Nice." She roughly pushed her hands through my hair and whispered harshly in my ear. "Nice. Nice. Nice." The bulbous tip of the dildo pressed against my belly then slid down to my impatient sex.

As if attempting to free myself, I squirmed. Renn stepped back and gave me a fast once-over. "Have you changed your mind? Is it dinner and the couch?"

I laughed. We both laughed. And that fast, Renn propped my legs around her waist and plunged the dildo into my resistant cunt.

"Whoa!" I muttered.

"Giddy-up," she cried. And boom. Boom. Boom. Boom. Boom. She danced, she bucked, she bobbed, she ducked. One-two. One-two.

I went up on that tool, down on that tool, up, down, up, down. My arms were fastened above my head, my legs were wrapped around her — up and down, up and down, she moved me and drew me, again and again.

She was sturdy, solid and firm. She swooped, she slammed. One-two. One-two. Boom, boom, boom.

I wanted more and more, this way and that. The dildo delved deep, plugging and rubbing against my pulsating cunt. With each fast plunge, I visualized myself pushed over a bench, taking it in the ass — wanting it, but not, begging for it, but not.

Into a come I started to teeter. And she lifted me, as if she knew, raised me high, as if she knew — and slowly, and slowly, as slow as she could, Renn lowered me down. Like a willing bull's eye, my ass slit seemed to open in heated anticipation. I could feel juice from my pussy dribbling down my crack, pooling near my ass rim. Like a blunted, swollen arrow, the dildo probed my tiny portal. Renn did a small jerk and the smooth head attempted entry into the crease.

I rode a fine line between burning pleasure and fear. I struggled between raising up, and slipping down. Renn did not stop. She tightened her grip and whispered in my ear, "Relax for me, baby. Just relax for me."

As the head pressed forward, the periphery of my ass seemed to tighten in concerned reluctance.

"That's it, Jennifer. Let me in, Jennifer. I'll go easy, baby. I'll be good to you, baby." Renn's words sizzled in my ear.

Down, I slid until the curved, bulky head cleaved into my teeny cave. Like a gentle invader, it penetrated into the tight dampness, splitting and caressing the virgin gate.

As if stirring from a dazed stupor, I opened my eyes. My arms were hoisted above my head and Renn was holding me firmly. Had she dug into every part of me? My back stung, my shoulders felt scraped and my tender ass throbbed. My entire body burned with a delicious, pulled-open-pushed-apart pleasure. Renn was panting. Sweat covered us both. Not certain when my last breath had been, I gasped for air and the foggy haze suddenly dissipated.

From the corner of my eye, I could see the mirror

beckoning. It was in that moment the unpleasant realization hit hard — that mirror, that wall-covering, full-length, ominous mirror would show *everything*. I was naked from the waist down. My arms were raised high. Would my thighs look thunderous or muscular? Would I look lanky or stout? Bottom line — was this a good mirror?

Refusing to ruin the mood, choosing not to dive into the grueling torture that self-appraisal in an unfamiliar mirror brings, I closed my eyes. But the nagging urge — *What harm? Just a glance? Aren't you curious?* — rode me hard.

It's the post-orgasm reflection that tells the truth. I knew that, we all knew that. Everyone looks good seconds before a climax — head thrown back in ecstasy, body tight with anticipation. Why hadn't I thought to assess myself then?

Just a glance. Aren't you curious? I opened my eyes, held my breath, and then jumped into the hazard of an unknown mirror. There I was — hair damp and flattened, face filled with pleasure — propped in the strong arms of a hard, attractive butch. A flood of relief swept through me. After all, in Renn's mirror, I looked pretty damn good.

RHINESTONE PUMPS

I have the shoes and am looking for you.
Iris, where are you?

I stole her shoes. I scooped them under my leather jacket and smuggled them out of the hotel room. Like I had robbed a fucking bank, I jumped on my bike and roared out of that lot without looking back. I stormed clear across town, shoes stuffed in my zipped jacket. Two blocks from home, a cop pulled me over. For a split second, I thought he was going to ask for the shoes, but he cited me for not wearing a helmet and sent me on my way. My heart pounded for the rest of the ride home.

My opinion? I deserved the shoes. If I had been

131

in an ordinary state of mind, I would have simply asked if I could have them as a souvenir. I'm sure *she* would have said yes. Her lover probably would have graced me with a why-not shrug and the shoes would have been mine, fair and square. But instead, without consent, I took the shoes.

Evidently, we had passed out on the bed. I awoke, sandwiched in between. Not wanting to disturb them, I slipped out of bed. It was after two. My clothes were scattered across the floor. Tangled in the post-sex high, I gathered my things. I felt groggy yet wired, hazy yet tightly wound.

I got dressed as quietly as possible. Certain that this sort of sex scene was best not hampered with good-byes, I hoped to sneak out the door without waking them. I put on my boots, buckled my belt and scanned the room for my leather jacket.

In the corner it lay in a crumpled pile. Next to it, her rhinestone-laden shoes sparkled seductively. Arched high on four-inch? five-inch? stiletto heels, they tapered to a severely pointed toe. They were just as provocative on their own as they had been on her feet.

I planned to put my coat on and head out the door but those shoes — those glittery, showy shoes — seemed to want more. As if they were directing, encouraging, urging me to take them along, I felt a bizarre compulsion to slide the sexy pumps under my jacket. One minute I was a good-time gal going home, the next, I was an outlaw, stealing a pair of shoes.

It had started innocently enough. Victim of a sudden window-shopping attack, I had stopped by the Castro on my way home from work. I saw her through a large storefront window. Dressed in a please-bend-over short black skirt and fishnet stockings, she was showing off a pair of thigh-high, patent leather boots. She did several runway-like turns while her lover, who dripped butch attitude, nodded in cool appreciation.

I, however, was less than subtle. Lust slammed me against the window. A loud thud ensued and both women did a fast-turn toward the window — and me.

They were attractive, but it was the miniskirted beauty in her up-the-leg boots that held my attention. Her young face was veiled behind painted red lips and lined-black eyes. Simultaneously, she seemed an innocent sixteen and a sly forty. All in one crazy, somersaulting moment, I wanted to seduce the virginal teenager and fuck the sultry woman — or fuck the untainted teen and seduce the fiery woman. Wild fantasies of how I would do it and how she would look tumbled over each other. Seconds later, I was in the store.

A young salesman was immediately at my side. "I'm looking for some bike boots," I muttered to him as I eyed her. "Size seven, men's."

He escorted me to a chair. As if intentional, the sex kitten slinked into the chair across from me. Her feline eyes said, *I want you to fuck me.* I flashed her an anytime grin. Her lover plopped into the seat next to her, concluding the insinuation with an over-my-dead-body smirk.

"Size seven it is." The salesman scurried to the back.

El Butcho shot me a cocksure smile and then kissed her woman. Falling into the embrace, the woman leaned back in her chair. As nonchalantly as possible, I glanced down to her uncrossed legs. The fishnets were secured with lacy garter straps — this I could see. The straps were stretched across her fleshy, white thighs — this I could see. But did she wear panties? It was a ravenous thirst for sociological knowledge, a deep desire to better understand the lesbian subculture, that compelled me to slowly slide down in my seat for a better, more reasonable view up that skirt. Would a woman like her — sporting a girlish smile and know-it-all eyes, dressed in fishnets and black garters — choose to wear panties? What progressive dyke in her right mind wouldn't want to know?

The lover continued her nonstop kisses and, caught in escalating curiosity, I slouched farther toward the floor. I peered up her skirt. It was dark — too dark, really — to know for sure about the panties. If only I had a flashlight . . . if only she'd spread her legs just a tiny, considerate bit more.

Lost in a cloud of reckless kisses, the woman opened her legs slightly, as if anticipating that one of us would certainly drop to her knees, separate those legs even wider, and suck her juicy clit right into one of our mouths. Trying to ascertain what was what up that uncooperative skirt, I had almost slithered all the way to the carpet.

"Here we are," the salesman interrupted. He had an armful of boxes. "I brought you several styles."

The women stopped kissing and turned their attention to me. Caught only inches from the floor, I awkwardly struggled back to the seat. My elbow banged on the wooden frame and a harsh electric-like sensation careened up my arm. The cry of pain launched in the back of my throat then smashed against my tightly clamped lips. I rubbed my elbow and glanced first at them and then at the salesman.

"Hard to stay in these damn chairs," I mumbled, smiling meekly. As though nothing out of the ordinary had transpired, as though we've all, on occasion, slid out of a chair, I reached for a pair of boots. "Great, thanks."

The woman giggled and flashed me another come-get-me smile. Her lover shot me an icy glare.

"Bad chairs," I offered with a stupid chuckle.

"Yeah, right," the lover breathed. Focused intently on me, her beady eyes were difficult to read — although the look suggested possible bone breakage ahead if I wasn't careful.

Attempting to gracefully dodge the intensity of her stare, I concentrated on my boot buckle, but even with my eyes diverted, I couldn't seem to escape the stronghold of El Butcho's gaze. Reluctantly, I glanced at her. To my surprise, she nodded. A butch nod is a quick, subtle movement. Hard to pinpoint and easy to miss. A thousand words can transpire in a simple tilt of the head. Slight as it was, I caught the gesture.

I regarded her cautiously. Her chestnut hair was shaved on the sides, full on top and long in the back. Her eyes had an erratic quality and her thin-lipped mouth was set in a perpetual sneer. I considered the chain tattooed around her neck and had to admit that it added a certain pitbull effect. A sudden desire to befriend rather than aggravate her overwhelmed me. Bottom line, she *was* pretty damned tough-looking — except for the silver studs decorating her jeans jacket. I snickered silently. What femme had talked her into that? I, on the other hand, knew what was what and only wore studs with leather. Pleased with myself, I reciprocated with a nod of my own — slight, subtle and butch.

The woman began removing one of her thigh-highs and the fix the lover and I had on each other snapped. I shoved my foot into a Made In USA bike boot. Across from me, the woman wrestled with hers. Her legs had parted, offering an exquisite view up her black miniskirt. Acting preoccupied with my own boots yet leaning heavy on peripheral vision, I strained to see. Jackpot! Red lace panties stretched tightly over the fat, curved bulge of her crotch.

The temptation to slide to the floor, to crawl across the carpet, to pull open her legs and rip her panties aside hounded me. Doing my best to stay in the chair, I forced my other foot into a boot.

I liked her red panties, oh God, I did. Her black garters sweetly contrasted with her creamy flesh. I was wet with desire, crazy for more. The fishnets sent a message, oh yes — so flirty, so easy, so ready. I liked her panties, her garters, her stockings. Hell, I liked *her*. From her spike-heeled boots, all the way up to her lace-trimmed pussy, she was my kind of woman every inch of the way. I wanted to stare, to linger hungrily on the delicious sight offered to me, but the thought of rocking my tenuous friendship with her mad-dog lover eased my attention from the red panties to the siren's face.

She had a stormy smile and lightning eyes. Her hair was coal black — or was it dyed deep blue? — the tint was intense and difficult to ascertain. Surely, if I had a better look, I'd see hair fringing the border of her panties and then I'd know the true color. Now that her lover and I had a better understanding, now

that we had nodded on equal ground, what harm
would there be in . . . ?

Had the lover just growled? In a fast jerk, I began
buckling the other boot. Black, blue, what did it
matter — her hair was lustrous, her skin like smooth
porcelain, and she looked good. She was mysterious, a
temptress. With a woman like her, it was difficult not
to think about spreading her legs, absurd not to
wonder about anonymous sex.

"Did you like the boots?" the lover asked in a low
tone.

Staring at my own feet, I waited for the woman's
reply. Silence.

"Did you like the boots?" the lover said again,
louder. I looked up to see her peering directly at me.

Was she talking to me? Did I like which boots? I
recalled the chain tattooed around her neck and made
the snap decision not to step on any toes. "Sure." I
shrugged, uncertain of a reply that would have
appeased her.

"Show her the other pair, Iris." The lover reached
for a covered box on the floor and passed it to the
woman. "Let's get an unbiased opinion."

Iris's eyes laughed as if to say, *You're going to
fuck me, all right.* The lover rested her hand on Iris's
thigh and they both smiled. And then, in a move as
graceful and alluring as a magician unveiling gems
from a bewitching scarf, Iris divided the magenta
tissue that lined the shoe box and revealed the
incredible rhinestone pumps.

Iris bought the glittery shoes . . . well, Iris chose

them and Marlee paid. Although Iris had looked spectacular in the thigh-high boots, there was something about those rhinestone pumps that left me absolutely breathless. Perhaps it was the far-reaching possibilities those shoes suggested — like Dorothy's ruby slippers in *The Wizard of Oz*. Simply wearing them made magic happen.

I imagined Iris wearing nothing but her silky black hose and frilly garters, elevated on those spiked heels, her full calves curved and tight. She'd click her heels and make her wish. *There's no place like home. There's no place like home.* Is home not where the heart is? *My* heart knew *exactly* where home was. Take me home, Iris. Hell . . . my eyes, my mouth, my fingers, all of me, knew what I called home. Right between her fishnetted legs was where I'd find my sanctuary. Take me home, Iris. Take me all the way home.

Iris wore the pumps out of the store. Arm in arm, she and Marlee strutted down the street. I followed after them, down Seventeenth to Castro. The shoes sparkled with each step Iris took — click, clack. Against the concrete the stiletto heels scraped — click, clack. Click, clack.

Marlee had laid out cash for the pumps, one hundred and eighty-three dollars. I couldn't blame her. I would have done the same. She took care of the transaction, leaving Iris and me alone at the chairs.

Iris fluttered her fiery eyes and sparks seemed to shoot around us both. "I really like those boots on you," she cooed.

"Yeah?" I glanced at my reflection in the mirror. I had a pair exactly like them at home.

"Buy them. They make me hot," she whispered.

She smiled. I smiled. She was still in the rhinestone pumps. Her tight pink sweater was poured over her breasts. I imagined her thick nipples waiting to be sucked. I could take her hand and pull her through the back door — was there a back door? — and to the parking lot. I'd pull that angora sweater over her breasts. I'd tug her red lace bra down. She'd have fat nipples, chunky nipples. I'd stroke them, squeeze them, ripple them up. Under her tiny black skirt, I'd push my hand. I'd rip those red panties, rip them right in half and press her against the dirty brick wall. Press her against the dirty brick wall and fuck her hard, like she'd never been fucked. Chain tattooed on a neck didn't mean anything when silver studs decorated a jeans jacket. I'd fuck her in leather. I'd fuck her right.

"Baby," Marlee called from the counter.

Iris smiled again and sashayed to Marlee's side. Seconds later, I was next to them, handing over one hundred and twenty hard-earned bucks on a pair of boots exactly like the ones at home. Sometimes, one has to skip past the unromantic realities of life due to extenuating circumstances — like Iris's young face, Iris's kohl-lined eyes, Iris's pert breasts, Iris's round ass. When one hasn't had sex in a while, overriding factors such as these take precedence over cash flow. An ordinary late afternoon, and Marlee and I had stood at the cash register, done our thing to please a femme.

Click. Clack. Click. Clack. They veered into a dingy alcove and through a wooden door. Smitten by those glistening shoes, entranced by the swish of Iris's hips, I stumbled along behind. Hadn't Marlee slapped me on the back and asked me to join them? Hadn't she and I butch-bonded when we spilt our twenties all over the counter? We were two of a kind, Marlee and I, swerving from the sidewalk into a bar.

Marlee pulled a fast butch move and paid for the drinks, but I evened the score when Iris pulled out a cigarette and needed a light. Not that I was interested in small-minded one-upmanship, but I had to keep some sense of respect. They headed for the dance floor and I wandered to the restroom. Locked in a stall, I hung my shoe bag on the hook, straddled the toilet and stared absently at the new boots that adorned my feet. One moment in a bar bathroom alone and sober brings hard reality right to the foreground. *What the hell was I doing with another pair of boots?*

Just then she knocked on the stall door. Just then I remembered why I had bought the boots.

"Can we talk privately?" she whispered.

Flustered, I yanked my jeans zipper and the sharp teeth caught my tender flesh. I didn't care — not when Iris was waiting for me. Should I just pull her into the stall when I opened the door? Yeah, I'd pull her into the stall, that's what I'd do. I'd lock us in and then kiss her like she'd never been kissed. I remembered her mouth — her saucy, pink mouth. I'd take her, I'd devour her, in one single kiss. I'd sit her on the toilet. I'd fall to my knees. She'd spread her legs for me, she'd show off those red panties. I'd take my time. I'd relish the view — the flimsy, delicate lace packing her succulent pussy lips into a

140

fat bulge, the feathery fringe of hairs skirting the panty border; the musk-scented wet spot.

She'd want it so bad that she'd pull those panties off herself. Moaning and squirming and grinding her hips, she'd try to tempt me into her throbbing treasures. Her lips would be full, flabby, thick. I'd separate them using both of my hands. Fold them back so that her beady little clit would stand out like a cherrystone.

I know about women — I know about her. Deep into her cleaved flesh, I'd dive with my tongue. She'd be sweet, she'd be fragrant, she'd be spun-sugar wet. Her pussy would engorge, would bloat, would enlarge. With my tongue, I'd lash her. With my fingers, I'd penetrate her.

"Well?" She knocked again.

"Sure. Sure. Sure," I muttered opening the door, expecting Iris but finding Marlee. Her eyes made brief contact with mine then shifted to my feet.

"Nice boots." Her tone was low-pitched but direct.

"Thanks." I glanced from her chain tattoo to her large hands and then on to my new boots.

"Iris likes them, too. But I suppose you already knew that —" She stepped closer, too close, really.

"She mentioned that . . . yeah . . ." I held my ground. After all, for a few hundred, I could have a chain tattooed around my neck, too.

"You like her shoes. She likes yours." Marlee was right in my face. The scent of Obsession for Men sucked the air from my lungs.

Butch reflex brought my hands to my hips. "What's this, a Vogue fashion report?"

"I think you know exactly what this is."

She had me there. I had no idea what the hell

this was. In that moment, I knew three things. One — I'd spent rent money on boots I already had. Two — she had asked me to join them for a drink. And three — I had already walked on concrete in the new shoes and wouldn't be able to take them back.

I shrugged, hoping she'd give me a clue.

"You want to fuck Iris."

Ding. I knew four things. And four, I wanted to fuck Iris. I considered the situation. If Marlee had come to confront me, drag me into a fight, wouldn't she already have my collar in her fist? Sure, the sneer was back on her face, but wasn't that perpetual? Hadn't she butch-buddied me with a nod, a slap on the back, an invitation to the party? Perhaps a situation such as this — two butch women bullshitting in a bathroom — warranted a certain amount of honesty.

"Well, now that you've mentioned it —" I didn't dare looked her straight in the eye. After all, this kind of discussion demanded all-out butch etiquette.

Marlee backed off. She peered at herself in the mirror, wet her hands and ran them through her hair. "You can't fuck her." With hair spiked higher, her mouth in that sneer, she had suddenly transformed from good ol' buddy to rabid dog.

"Course not," I said faintly. What had I been thinking? Had I really imagined this rottweiler butch was going to hand me her woman on a silver platter — *Here, fuck her, have a good time. Call me when you're done*? I cringed, expecting her to turn, slam me against the wall and tear out my throat. Should I hit her first? Duck and run? Act nonchalant?

"But you can watch." Marlee finished with her

hair and turned back to me. Water sprinkled from her hands to the floor. "You can watch how it comes down. Iris is hot. She's wild. You interested in that?"

I suddenly realized that I wasn't breathing and gasped for air. "Well ... I ... well ... yes ... I suppose ..."

"You like the rhinestone shoes? Wait till you see me fuck her with one of those thin, spiked heels." She pulled open the bathroom door and disappeared into the bar.

I wiped a splotch of water from the toe of my brand-new boot and took a moment to congratulate myself on the best hundred bucks I'd ever spent.

We had a couple drinks at the bar but Marlee's proposal wasn't discussed. Marlee was all over Iris, kissing her, biting her neck, rubbing her breasts. I could distinctly see the contour of Iris's nipples, erect and desperate, protruding beneath her sweater. Like a contented cat, Iris arched toward Marlee with each caress, but all the while, she gazed at me. She wanted me to fuck her. Her desire for me snapped in her eyes.

Marlee suddenly pulled back and turned to me. "Let's head for the room. You may as well ride over with us. I'll get you there and back."

"We've rented a great car," Iris added. "Marlee can be our chauffeur and you and I can sit in the back." Hot as the tropics, Iris was hard to resist. I wondered if Marlee had mentioned the teensy detail she had shared with me in the bathroom about who would and wouldn't be fucking Iris?

Going to a hotel to watch a stranger get fucked with a rhinestone shoe was one thing. But when the butch says you're only watching and the femme pleads to get fucked — things could get touchy. The vision of Marlee driving me back, teeth bared, fingers in an angry grip on the steering wheel, was not a pretty one. Preferring the flexibility of a moment's-notice exit, I rode my bike and met them at the room.

They were from Atlanta. Mixing business with pleasure, this was their last night in San Francisco. Obviously, having a guest was a last-minute decision — the floor was covered with opened suitcases and clothes were hanging over all the chairs.

"We were packing. Sorry about the mess." Iris fluttered around the room, closing suitcases and moving piles of clothes.

I had fantasized about her on my ride to the hotel — how she'd look naked, how she'd look with her long legs spread and her pussy split apart. Would Marlee allow me a close look or would I be required to sit across the room? There was the queen size bed in one corner and a table and two chairs in the other. The chairs were too far from the bed to suit my needs. If I could move a chair to the edge of the bed, well, then, yes, then we'd have a real party.

Marlee came out of the bathroom with a tape player under her arm. She set it on the table and plugged it in. "Shot of whiskey?" She grabbed a fifth from the dresser and pulled the cork with her teeth.

"Nah." I shook my head.

Marlee offered me the bottle anyway. "Aw, c'mon. One swig. It'll loosen you up."

Iris intercepted. "Let me have it first," she

purred, grabbing the whiskey. "I'll have you both loosened up in seconds."

With a pleased smirk, Marlee relinquished the bottle. She clicked on a tape then motioned to a chair. "You sit here."

"In the corner?" I said sourly.

Iris flashed me a look that could melt snowcaps. I sat down.

"And don't get up," Marlee said sternly. She took the bottle from Iris and set it on the floor.

And Iris — oh Iris — began swaying to the music. She rotated her hips. The short skirt flirted with the black trim of her fishnets. Slowly, carefully, she slid each pearl button through the eyelets on her soft, pink sweater. I was seconds away from finding out about those nipples, those hard, red nipples.

The sweater opened. The red lace bra pushed her small breasts into high, voluptuous curves. The arc of her darkened areola teased against the bra. Iris danced without taking a step. Gyrating her full hips, she let her sweater drop to the floor. How delicate her body was. She was slender. She was small.

Unable to tear my eyes from the delectable plushness of her breasts, I lustfully strained to see a hint of her contracted nipple under the lace. Yes, oh yes — she pulled a strap from her shoulder. Yes. Yes. She pulled the other.

Marlee danced her way over to Iris. "So beautiful. So beautiful," she hissed. And she was right. Her strong hand grabbed around Iris's waist. As if depending only on Marlee's grip, Iris arched back, letting her hands fall to her sides. Marlee tugged the bra down and Iris's berry nipples came into view. A demanding ache in my cunt caused me to jerk in my chair. I wanted so much to push Marlee aside, to take Iris in my arms, to hold her while she leaned back. I'd press my hands up and down her distended nipples. I'd sway and twist and . . .

The music was steamy, dark. The continual beat kept a driving force. Yes. Oh yes. Marlee sucked Iris's erect nipple into her mouth. Iris moaned. A wave of pleasure graced her face. Marlee pulled back to reveal that the plum-tinted knot had doubled in size.

"Pretty, huh," Marlee muttered to me.

"Yes," I whispered. "Pretty."

Marlee unzipped Iris's skirt. I thought about those red panties, that thickened crotch area. What kind of a pussy did Iris have? Would they let me move closer? Would they? I grabbed the arms of the chair and leaned, leaned, leaned forward. The chair, as if it had a mind of its own, moved an inch toward them. I didn't resist.

Marlee stepped back. The skirt dropped to the floor. Iris continued her sensual dance. I rode the music, raced the music, down into the shadows of an unexplored cave. Tiny candle flames flickered in the darkness and nothing more. Enigma. Yes, the music was Enigma. Iris and I, deep in a cave, would sail the music of Enigma further down.

Her waist was small, her hips full. She had thighs that were meant to be spread. An ass that was meant to be grabbed. The chair inched forward and I willingly went along.

The panties fell to the floor. Iris's pussy was trimmed like a showgirl's. A sparse strip of jet-black hair covered her bunched lips. Iris weaved her fingers into that hair. Her head was tossed back, her eyes were closed. And lower, lower, lower, she squatted.

Her pussy brushed the lip of the whiskey bottle. To the music, she swiveled. To the music, I watched the curved head of the bottle disappear into her marvelous sex. She lifted slightly, then slid down, fucking that bottle repeatedly. The chair crept forward. The chair crept forward again, then again.

Iris smiled and the room blazed orange-red. Up and down. Up and down, she glided on that smooth, cool glass. In a cave, she and I. Deep into the womb of the earth, we forged. The rhinestone pumps glittered like illuminated stalagmites. Like diamonds spilt across a mine shaft floor, the rhinestone shoes entranced. Further and further, I followed her into the darkness of desire. There was something about Iris that grabbed hold of me and wouldn't let go. More than sex, more than lust, she was like a goddess, a source of something deep within. A well? An underwater stream? Iris and I, only Iris and I, heading to the place where the earth's blood flows . . .

Iris raised herself from the squat and the bottle stayed clamped in her pussy. Marlee — *what the hell was she still doing here?* — plucked the bottle from between Iris's legs. "Drink?" she passed me the whiskey. Its neck was iced with white spice. I took that bottle. I took that bottle and pushed it into my mouth. I licked it. I sucked it. I lapped every drop of her sacred juice.

And the chair, on its own, crept closer. Marlee lifted Iris and laid her on the bed. Iris — in garters, stockings and rhinestone shoes. *There is no place like home. There is no place like home.*

"Do you want to see now?" Iris's legs were bent. The thin, stiletto heels pierced sharply into the bed.

Marlee pulled a shoe off Iris's foot. "Should we

show her, Cinderella? Should we show her the way you really like to get fucked?"

Iris seemed lost in herself and did not speak. Instead she let her knees fall as far as they could toward each side of the bed. Her magnificent pussy flapped open for me to see it all. Her outer lips were large, her inner lips dangled like pink curtains over her slit. Like a spongy sac of pink folds, her clitoral flesh jutted forward. Iris reached down and pulled her cunt, exposing her clit-tip, which pushed out like a tiny spring bud.

The tension caused the smaller lips to spread, revealing a small, pulsating opening. Beads of sex oil pooled on the thickened rim. The chair moved closer, I didn't protest. Sweet, glossy, satiny beads — if I could just dip one finger, slice one finger into her sap and draw it up and over that rosebud clit — just once and I'd be satisfied.

Marlee traced the compact tip of the heel along the circumference of Iris's jewel box. As if trying not to waste time getting that spike into her cunt, Iris lunged. She continued to grind her hips to the music. Deeper and deeper, riding the beat — I'd follow her anywhere. To the depths of darkness, to the underworld's heated pit.

Marlee dragged the heel in little circles along the raised, reddened flesh. Sex cream covered the tip and Marlee trailed it up to the maroon-tinted clit bead. Carefully, gently, she tapped against the erect pleasure-point.

Iris was writhing in ecstasy. At the edge of the bed, Marlee, the chair and I huddled. I could see it all. That heel, that spiked rhinestone heel tapped and tapped and tapped her clit.

"Fuck her," I said. My voice was gruff, almost unrecognizable.

"Yeah?" Marlee grunted.

"Yeah, fuck her with the shoe."

Marlee pulled a condom from her pocket, ripped the package with her teeth and sheathed the long, tapered heel. Without thought, without consideration — I pushed her hand back to the slit and watched in delirious awe as that spiked heel, that four-inch heel, sank right into her cunt.

"Marlee, baby. Mar — fuck me good. Fuck me good. So, like so — Only you. It's there —" Iris's words began to melt into each other.

Marlee was on the bed, I was off the chair, Iris was who knows where, and the shoe was being swallowed by her throbbing slit. In and out, I pushed Marlee's hand. I could see the pussy muscles grasping hungrily at the shoe, trying to hold it, to keep the smooth stalk from totally disengaging.

And then Marlee grabbed me, pulled me onto the bed. I reached for Iris, prayed for Iris, fell into Iris with my hands, my mouth, my teeth, my lips. She kissed me. She cried my name. Into the abyss, into unknown chambers deep in the earth — the place where only goddesses and women can find their way — that's where she took me. That's where we went.

Iris and me. Just Iris and me. It got darker. It got deeper. Wild fires burned heavy and hard. Into Iris, again and again — the rhinestone pump, that lovely, shimmering rhinestone pump — plunged relentlessly.

* * * * *

I stole the shoes. I scooped them under my leather jacket and smuggled them out of the room. On my dresser, for over two weeks, they've sat. All I can think of is Iris and the passageways she swept me through. I'm looking for her. I've placed an ad in the *Southern Voice* and I won't cancel it until I find her. Iris, sweet Iris. I'm looking for Iris. All I can think of is Iris. Many times, behind closed doors, I've stuffed my feet in those rhinestone pumps and whispered, "There's no place like home. There's no place like home." Sometimes magic happens just with a wish.

Iris, where are you?

IN THE BLINK OF AN EYE

A sudden crack startles me. She is standing by the bed, anger riding her face like an oncoming thunderstorm. "And you just fall back to sleep! Just like that! Without a care?" Her glass-sliver words slice. "Did you even look at the places I circled?"

I sit up and push the newspaper aside. "No." I am groggy and confused. Dream fragments glide between her words like silvery fish. *There is no place like home. There is no place like home.*

"No?" Lightning flares in her eyes and the storm blows closer. *"No?"*

"No." I shake my head and reach for her, all in one movement. "I'm so sorry, Vivian. I can change. Really."

She steps back and studies me carefully. A tear balances on her lash. I sense a door closing. A thin slit is what's left to slip through to her.

"I don't think so." She turns to leave.

This is my last chance. On the edge of a purple-vined well, I teeter, debating. *Can I really change?* "Vivian, please?"

"Please what?" She whirls around. "Please give you one more chance? So you can work late and not be home and....and..." She bursts into tears.

In that moment, the reality of how she has missed me, of how I've missed her, hits hard. I climb out of bed and go to her. She is soft and fragile in my arms. I wonder why it was so hard to be here. I wonder why I had feared her closeness.

Tears spill from her eyes and dampen my cheek. Dear God, she is everything to me. Like white-water rapids, emotions rage through me. Our tears mix. Sad love smears our faces. The helix of agonizing grief and desperate love turns, digging deep into my heart. Why had I worked such long hours? Stayed away? Left her home by herself every night?

My lips find hers and I'm drawn into the lushness of her kiss. Falling into her magic, I close my eyes, I let go. Lost in the plushness of her breasts, her hips, her ass, I disappear from myself. I caress her luscious breasts. Her nipples tighten into square pellets. She moans. I moan. Tears stream. This, right here, is where I need to be. I love her. I love her so much. Down snow-covered mountain slopes, I slide with her. Across flower-drenched fields, through a kaleidoscope of blooming colors, I run with her. We soar in star-studded darkness, ride racing wild winds.

She is the sultry summer night, autumn's colored leaves. The warmth of a winter cabin fire, this is her. When she lets me love her, I become these things through her. I anticipate the summers, embrace the winters.

"Please, please, Vivian?" I mutter, my lips pressed against her neck. In a waterfall of passion, we cascade to the bed. Her perfume is sweet ambrosia. I kiss her again and again. Her nipples are firm under my fingers. Her body presses into mine. Is there anything as graceful, as powerful as two women in love? Volcano goddess steps forward. Neptune backs down. There is nothing as powerful as this.

And will I change for her? Will I come home and drink from the well, trusting that I'll be safe, trusting that I can protect her, too? My fingers slide across the curve of her belly and into her pajama bottoms. She cries. I cry. And down, into her softness, I go. Like a roller-coaster dream, like a dancer with fire . . . and down and down and down I go. Home. To her.

In the blink of an eye, all this, and more.

A few of the publications of
THE NAIAD PRESS, INC.
P.O. Box 10543 • Tallahassee, Florida 32302
Phone (904) 539-5965
Toll-Free Order Number: 1-800-533-1973
Mail orders welcome. Please include 15% postage.
Write or call for our free catalog which also features an
incredible selection of lesbian videos.

COSTA BRAVA by Marta Balletbo Coll. 144 pp. Read the book, see the movie! ISBN 1-56280-153-8 $11.95

MEETING MAGDALENE & OTHER STORIES by Marilyn Freeman. 160 pp. Read the book, see the movie! ISBN 1-56280-170-8 11.95

SECOND FIDDLE by Kate Calloway. 240 pp. P.I. Cassidy James' second case. ISBN 1-56280-169-6 11.95

LAUREL by Isabel Miller. 128 pp. By the author of the beloved *Patience and Sarah.* ISBN 1-56280-146-5 10.95

LOVE OR MONEY by Jackie Calhoun. 240 pp. The romance of real life. ISBN 1-56280-147-3 10.95

SMOKE AND MIRRORS by Pat Welch. 224 pp. 5th Helen Black Mystery. ISBN 1-56280-143-0 10.95

DANCING IN THE DARK edited by Barbara Grier & Christine Cassidy. 272 pp. Erotic love stories by Naiad Press authors. ISBN 1-56280-144-9 14.95

TIME AND TIME AGAIN by Catherine Ennis. 176 pp. Passionate love affair. ISBN 1-56280-145-7 10.95

PAXTON COURT by Diane Salvatore. 256 pp. Erotic and wickedly funny contemporary tale about the business of learning to live together. ISBN 1-56280-114-7 10.95

INNER CIRCLE by Claire McNab. 208 pp. 8th Carol Ashton Mystery. ISBN 1-56280-135-X 10.95

LESBIAN SEX: AN ORAL HISTORY by Susan Johnson. 240 pp. Need we say more? ISBN 1-56280-142-2 14.95

BABY, IT'S COLD by Jaye Maiman. 256 pp. 5th Robin Miller Mystery. ISBN 1-56280-141-4 19.95

WILD THINGS by Karin Kallmaker. 240 pp. By the undisputed mistress of lesbian romance. ISBN 1-56280-139-2 10.95

THE GIRL NEXT DOOR by Mindy Kaplan. 208 pp. Just what
you'd expect. ISBN 1-56280-140-6 10.95

NOW AND THEN by Penny Hayes. 240 pp. Romance on the
westward journey. ISBN 1-56280-121-X 10.95

HEART ON FIRE by Diana Simmonds. 176 pp. The romantic and
erotic rival of *Curious Wine*. ISBN 1-56280-152-X 10.95

DEATH AT LAVENDER BAY by Lauren Wright Douglas. 208 pp.
1st Allison O'Neil Mystery. ISBN 1-56280-085-X 10.95

YES I SAID YES I WILL by Judith McDaniel. 272 pp. Hot
romance by famous author. ISBN 1-56280-138-4 10.95

FORBIDDEN FIRES by Margaret C. Anderson. Edited by Mathilda
Hills. 176 pp. Famous author's "unpublished" Lesbian romance.
ISBN 1-56280-123-6 21.95

SIDE TRACKS by Teresa Stores. 160 pp. Gender-bending
Lesbians on the road. ISBN 1-56280-122-8 10.95

HOODED MURDER by Annette Van Dyke. 176 pp. 1st Jessie
Batelle Mystery. ISBN 1-56280-134-1 10.95

WILDWOOD FLOWERS by Julia Watts. 208 pp. Hilarious and
heart-warming tale of true love. ISBN 1-56280-127-9 10.95

NEVER SAY NEVER by Linda Hill. 224 pp. Rule #1: Never get involved
with . . . ISBN 1-56280-126-0 10.95

THE SEARCH by Melanie McAllester. 240 pp. Exciting top cop
Tenny Mendoza case. ISBN 1-56280-150-3 10.95

THE WISH LIST by Saxon Bennett. 192 pp. Romance through
the years. ISBN 1-56280-125-2 10.95

FIRST IMPRESSIONS by Kate Calloway. 208 pp. P.I. Cassidy
James' first case. ISBN 1-56280-133-3 10.95

OUT OF THE NIGHT by Kris Bruyer. 192 pp. Spine-tingling
thriller. ISBN 1-56280-120-1 10.95

NORTHERN BLUE by Tracey Richardson. 224 pp. Police recruits
Miki & Miranda — passion in the line of fire. ISBN 1-56280-118-X 10.95

LOVE'S HARVEST by Peggy J. Herring. 176 pp. by the author of
Once More With Feeling. ISBN 1-56280-117-1 10.95

THE COLOR OF WINTER by Lisa Shapiro. 208 pp. Romantic
love beyond your wildest dreams. ISBN 1-56280-116-3 10.95

FAMILY SECRETS by Laura DeHart Young. 208 pp. Enthralling
romance and suspense. ISBN 1-56280-119-8 10.95

INLAND PASSAGE by Jane Rule. 288 pp. Tales exploring conven-
tional & unconventional relationships. ISBN 0-930044-56-8 10.95

DOUBLE BLUFF by Claire McNab. 208 pp. 7th Carol Ashton
Mystery. ISBN 1-56280-096-5 10.95

BAR GIRLS by Lauran Hoffman. 176 pp. See the movie, read the book! ISBN 1-56280-115-5   10.95

THE FIRST TIME EVER edited by Barbara Grier & Christine Cassidy. 272 pp. Love stories by Naiad Press authors. ISBN 1-56280-086-8   14.95

MISS PETTIBONE AND MISS McGRAW by Brenda Weathers. 208 pp. A charming ghostly love story. ISBN 1-56280-151-1   10.95

CHANGES by Jackie Calhoun. 208 pp. Involved romance and relationships. ISBN 1-56280-083-3   10.95

FAIR PLAY by Rose Beecham. 256 pp. 3rd Amanda Valentine Mystery. ISBN 1-56280-081-7   10.95

PAYBACK by Celia Cohen. 176 pp. A gripping thriller of romance, revenge and betrayal. ISBN 1-56280-084-1   10.95

THE BEACH AFFAIR by Barbara Johnson. 224 pp. Sizzling summer romance/mystery/intrigue. ISBN 1-56280-090-6   10.95

GETTING THERE by Robbi Sommers. 192 pp. Nobody does it like Robbi! ISBN 1-56280-099-X   10.95

FINAL CUT by Lisa Haddock. 208 pp. 2nd Carmen Ramirez Mystery. ISBN 1-56280-088-4   10.95

FLASHPOINT by Katherine V. Forrest. 256 pp. A Lesbian blockbuster! ISBN 1-56280-079-5   10.95

CLAIRE OF THE MOON by Nicole Conn. Audio Book —Read by Marianne Hyatt. ISBN 1-56280-113-9   16.95

FOR LOVE AND FOR LIFE: INTIMATE PORTRAITS OF LESBIAN COUPLES by Susan Johnson. 224 pp. ISBN 1-56280-091-4   14.95

DEVOTION by Mindy Kaplan. 192 pp. See the movie — read the book! ISBN 1-56280-093-0   10.95

SOMEONE TO WATCH by Jaye Maiman. 272 pp. 4th Robin Miller Mystery. ISBN 1-56280-095-7   10.95

GREENER THAN GRASS by Jennifer Fulton. 208 pp. A young woman — a stranger in her bed. ISBN 1-56280-092-2   10.95

TRAVELS WITH DIANA HUNTER by Regine Sands. Erotic lesbian romp. Audio Book (2 cassettes) ISBN 1-56280-107-4   16.95

CABIN FEVER by Carol Schmidt. 256 pp. Sizzling suspense and passion. ISBN 1-56280-089-1   10.95

THERE WILL BE NO GOODBYES by Laura DeHart Young. 192 pp. Romantic love, strength, and friendship. ISBN 1-56280-103-1   10.95

FAULTLINE by Sheila Ortiz Taylor. 144 pp. Joyous comic lesbian novel. ISBN 1-56280-108-2   9.95

OPEN HOUSE by Pat Welch. 176 pp. 4th Helen Black Mystery. ISBN 1-56280-102-3   10.95

ONCE MORE WITH FEELING by Peggy J. Herring. 240 pp.
Lighthearted, loving romantic adventure.   ISBN 1-56280-089-2   10.95

FOREVER by Evelyn Kennedy. 224 pp. Passionate romance — love
overcoming all obstacles.   ISBN 1-56280-094-9   10.95

WHISPERS by Kris Bruyer. 176 pp. Romantic ghost story
ISBN 1-56280-082-5   10.95

NIGHT SONGS by Penny Mickelbury. 224 pp. 2nd Gianna Maglione
Mystery.   ISBN 1-56280-097-3   10.95

GETTING TO THE POINT by Teresa Stores. 256 pp. Classic
southern Lesbian novel.   ISBN 1-56280-100-7   10.95

PAINTED MOON by Karin Kallmaker. 224 pp. Delicious
Kallmaker romance.   ISBN 1-56280-075-2   10.95

THE MYSTERIOUS NAIAD edited by Katherine V. Forrest &
Barbara Grier. 320 pp. Love stories by Naiad Press authors.
ISBN 1-56280-074-4   14.95

DAUGHTERS OF A CORAL DAWN by Katherine V. Forrest.
240 pp. Tenth Anniversay Edition.   ISBN 1-56280-104-X   10.95

BODY GUARD by Claire McNab. 208 pp. 6th Carol Ashton
Mystery.   ISBN 1-56280-073-6   10.95

CACTUS LOVE by Lee Lynch. 192 pp. Stories by the beloved
storyteller.   ISBN 1-56280-071-X   9.95

SECOND GUESS by Rose Beecham. 216 pp. 2nd Amanda Valentine
Mystery.   ISBN 1-56280-069-8   9.95

A RAGE OF MAIDENS by Lauren Wright Douglas. 240 pp. 6th Caitlin
Reece Mystery.   ISBN 1-56280-068-X   10.95

TRIPLE EXPOSURE by Jackie Calhoun. 224 pp. Romantic drama
involving many characters.   ISBN 1-56280-067-1   10.95

UP, UP AND AWAY by Catherine Ennis. 192 pp. Delightful
romance.   ISBN 1-56280-065-5   9.95

PERSONAL ADS by Robbi Sommers. 176 pp. Sizzling short
stories.   ISBN 1-56280-059-0   10.95

CROSSWORDS by Penny Sumner. 256 pp. 2nd Victoria Cross
Mystery.   ISBN 1-56280-064-7   9.95

SWEET CHERRY WINE by Carol Schmidt. 224 pp. A novel of
suspense.   ISBN 1-56280-063-9   9.95

CERTAIN SMILES by Dorothy Tell. 160 pp. Erotic short stories.
ISBN 1-56280-066-3   9.95

EDITED OUT by Lisa Haddock. 224 pp. 1st Carmen Ramirez
Mystery.   ISBN 1-56280-077-9   9.95

WEDNESDAY NIGHTS by Camarin Grae. 288 pp. Sexy
adventure.   ISBN 1-56280-060-4   10.95

SMOKEY O by Celia Cohen. 176 pp. Relationships on the
playing field. ISBN 1-56280-057-4   9.95

KATHLEEN O'DONALD by Penny Hayes. 256 pp. Rose and
Kathleen find each other and employment in 1909 NYC.
ISBN 1-56280-070-1   9.95

STAYING HOME by Elisabeth Nonas. 256 pp. Molly and Alix
want a baby . . . or do they? ISBN 1-56280-076-0   10.95

TRUE LOVE by Jennifer Fulton. 240 pp. Six lesbians searching
for love in all the "right" places. ISBN 1-56280-035-3   10.95

KEEPING SECRETS by Penny Mickelbury. 208 pp. 1st Gianna
Maglione Mystery. ISBN 1-56280-052-3   9.95

THE ROMANTIC NAIAD edited by Katherine V. Forrest &
Barbara Grier. 336 pp. Love stories by Naiad Press authors.
ISBN 1-56280-054-X   14.95

UNDER MY SKIN by Jaye Maiman. 336 pp. 3rd Robin Miller
Mystery. ISBN 1-56280-049-3.   10.95

CAR POOL by Karin Kallmaker. 272pp. Lesbians on wheels
and then some! ISBN 1-56280-048-5   10.95

NOT TELLING MOTHER: STORIES FROM A LIFE by Diane
Salvatore. 176 pp. Her 3rd novel. ISBN 1-56280-044-2   9.95

GOBLIN MARKET by Lauren Wright Douglas. 240pp. 5th Caitlin
Reece Mystery. ISBN 1-56280-047-7   10.95

LONG GOODBYES by Nikki Baker. 256 pp. 3rd Virginia Kelly
Mystery. ISBN 1-56280-042-6   9.95

FRIENDS AND LOVERS by Jackie Calhoun. 224 pp. Mid-
western Lesbian lives and loves. ISBN 1-56280-041-8   10.95

THE CAT CAME BACK by Hilary Mullins. 208 pp. Highly
praised Lesbian novel. ISBN 1-56280-040-X   9.95

BEHIND CLOSED DOORS by Robbi Sommers. 192 pp. Hot,
erotic short stories. ISBN 1-56280-039-6   9.95

CLAIRE OF THE MOON by Nicole Conn. 192 pp. See the
movie — read the book! ISBN 1-56280-038-8   10.95

SILENT HEART by Claire McNab. 192 pp. Exotic Lesbian
romance. ISBN 1-56280-036-1   10.95

THE SPY IN QUESTION by Amanda Kyle Williams. 256 pp.
4th Madison McGuire Mystery. ISBN 1-56280-037-X   9.95

SAVING GRACE by Jennifer Fulton. 240 pp. Adventure and
romantic entanglement. ISBN 1-56280-051-5   10.95

CURIOUS WINE by Katherine V. Forrest. 176 pp. Tenth Anniver-
sary Edition. The most popular contemporary Lesbian love story.
ISBN 1-56280-053-1   10.95
　　　　Audio Book (2 cassettes) ISBN 1-56280-105-8   16.95

CHAUTAUQUA by Catherine Ennis. 192 pp. Exciting, romantic
adventure. ISBN 1-56280-032-9 9.95

A PROPER BURIAL by Pat Welch. 192 pp. 3rd Helen Black
Mystery. ISBN 1-56280-033-7 9.95

SILVERLAKE HEAT: A Novel of Suspense by Carol Schmidt.
240 pp. Rhonda is as hot as Laney's dreams. ISBN 1-56280-031-0 9.95

LOVE, ZENA BETH by Diane Salvatore. 224 pp. The most talked
about lesbian novel of the nineties! ISBN 1-56280-030-2 10.95

A DOORYARD FULL OF FLOWERS by Isabel Miller. 160 pp.
Stories incl. 2 sequels to *Patience and Sarah.* ISBN 1-56280-029-9 9.95

MURDER BY TRADITION by Katherine V. Forrest. 288 pp. 4th
Kate Delafield Mystery. ISBN 1-56280-002-7 11.95

THE EROTIC NAIAD edited by Katherine V. Forrest & Barbara
Grier. 224 pp. Love stories by Naiad Press authors.
ISBN 1-56280-026-4 14.95

DEAD CERTAIN by Claire McNab. 224 pp. 5th Carol Ashton
Mystery. ISBN 1-56280-027-2 10.95

CRAZY FOR LOVING by Jaye Maiman. 320 pp. 2nd Robin Miller
Mystery. ISBN 1-56280-025-6 10.95

STONEHURST by Barbara Johnson. 176 pp. Passionate regency
romance. ISBN 1-56280-024-8 9.95

INTRODUCING AMANDA VALENTINE by Rose Beecham.
256 pp. 1st Amanda Valentine Mystery. ISBN 1-56280-021-3 10.95

UNCERTAIN COMPANIONS by Robbi Sommers. 204 pp.
Steamy, erotic novel. ISBN 1-56280-017-5 9.95

A TIGER'S HEART by Lauren W. Douglas. 240 pp. 4th Caitlin
Reece Mystery. ISBN 1-56280-018-3 9.95

PAPERBACK ROMANCE by Karin Kallmaker. 256 pp. A
delicious romance. ISBN 1-56280-019-1 10.95

THE LAVENDER HOUSE MURDER by Nikki Baker. 224 pp.
2nd Virginia Kelly Mystery. ISBN 1-56280-012-4 9.95

PASSION BAY by Jennifer Fulton. 224 pp. Passionate romance,
virgin beaches, tropical skies. ISBN 1-56280-028-0 10.95

STICKS AND STONES by Jackie Calhoun. 208 pp. Contemporary
lesbian lives and loves. ISBN 1-56280-020-5 9.95
Audio Book (2 cassettes) ISBN 1-56280-106-6 16.95

UNDER THE SOUTHERN CROSS by Claire McNab. 192 pp.
Romantic nights Down Under. ISBN 1-56280-011-6 9.95

GRASSY FLATS by Penny Hayes. 256 pp. Lesbian romance in
the '30s. ISBN 1-56280-010-8 9.95

A SINGULAR SPY by Amanda K. Williams. 192 pp. 3rd
Madison McGuire Mystery. ISBN 1-56280-008-6 8.95

THE END OF APRIL by Penny Sumner. 240 pp. 1st Victoria
Cross Mystery. ISBN 1-56280-007-8   8.95

KISS AND TELL by Robbi Sommers. 192 pp. Scorching stories
by the author of *Pleasures.* ISBN 1-56280-005-1   10.95

STILL WATERS by Pat Welch. 208 pp. 2nd Helen Black Mystery.
ISBN 0-941483-97-5   9.95

TO LOVE AGAIN by Evelyn Kennedy. 208 pp. Wildly romantic
love story. ISBN 0-941483-85-1   9.95

IN THE GAME by Nikki Baker. 192 pp. 1st Virginia Kelly
Mystery. ISBN 1-56280-004-3   9.95

STRANDED by Camarin Grae. 320 pp. Entertaining, riveting
adventure. ISBN 0-941483-99-1   9.95

THE DAUGHTERS OF ARTEMIS by Lauren Wright Douglas.
240 pp. 3rd Caitlin Reece Mystery. ISBN 0-941483-95-9   9.95

CLEARWATER by Catherine Ennis. 176 pp. Romantic secrets
of a small Louisiana town. ISBN 0-941483-65-7   8.95

THE HALLELUJAH MURDERS by Dorothy Tell. 176 pp. 2nd
Poppy Dillworth Mystery. ISBN 0-941483-88-6   8.95

SECOND CHANCE by Jackie Calhoun. 256 pp. Contemporary
Lesbian lives and loves. ISBN 0-941483-93-2   9.95

BENEDICTION by Diane Salvatore. 272 pp. Striking, contemporary romantic novel. ISBN 0-941483-90-8   10.95

TOUCHWOOD by Karin Kallmaker. 240 pp. Loving, May/
December romance. ISBN 0-941483-76-2   9.95

COP OUT by Claire McNab. 208 pp. 4th Carol Ashton Mystery.
ISBN 0-941483-84-3   10.95

THE BEVERLY MALIBU by Katherine V. Forrest. 288 pp. 3rd
Kate Delafield Mystery. ISBN 0-941483-48-7   11.95

THE PROVIDENCE FILE by Amanda Kyle Williams. 256 pp.
2nd Madison McGuire Mystery. ISBN 0-941483-92-4   8.95

I LEFT MY HEART by Jaye Maiman. 320 pp. 1st Robin Miller
Mystery. ISBN 0-941483-72-X   10.95

THE PRICE OF SALT by Patricia Highsmith (writing as Claire
Morgan). 288 pp. Classic lesbian novel, first issued in 1952 . . .
acknowledged by its author under her own, very famous, name.
ISBN 1-56280-003-5   10.95

SIDE BY SIDE by Isabel Miller. 256 pp. From beloved author of
Patience and Sarah. ISBN 0-941483-77-0   10.95

STAYING POWER: LONG TERM LESBIAN COUPLES by
Susan E. Johnson. 352 pp. Joys of coupledom. ISBN 0-941-483-75-4   14.95

SLICK by Camarin Grae. 304 pp. Exotic, erotic adventure.
ISBN 0-941483-74-6   9.95

NINTH LIFE by Lauren Wright Douglas. 256 pp. 2nd Caitlin
Reece Mystery. ISBN 0-941483-50-9 9.95

PLAYERS by Robbi Sommers. 192 pp. Sizzling, erotic novel.
ISBN 0-941483-73-8 9.95

MURDER AT RED ROOK RANCH by Dorothy Tell. 224 pp.
1st Poppy Dillworth Mystery. ISBN 0-941483-80-0 8.95

A ROOM FULL OF WOMEN by Elisabeth Nonas. 256 pp.
Contemporary Lesbian lives. ISBN 0-941483-69-X 9.95

THEME FOR DIVERSE INSTRUMENTS by Jane Rule. 208 pp.
Powerful romantic lesbian stories. ISBN 0-941483-63-0 8.95

CLUB 12 by Amanda Kyle Williams. 288 pp. Espionage thriller
featuring a lesbian agent! ISBN 0-941483-64-9 9.95

DEATH DOWN UNDER by Claire McNab. 240 pp. 3rd Carol
Ashton Mystery. ISBN 0-941483-39-8 10.95

MONTANA FEATHERS by Penny Hayes. 256 pp. Vivian and
Elizabeth find love in frontier Montana. ISBN 0-941483-61-4 9.95

LIFESTYLES by Jackie Calhoun. 224 pp. Contemporary Lesbian
lives and loves. ISBN 0-941483-57-6 10.95

WILDERNESS TREK by Dorothy Tell. 192 pp. Six women on
vacation learning ''new'' skills. ISBN 0-941483-60-6 8.95

MURDER BY THE BOOK by Pat Welch. 256 pp. 1st Helen
Black Mystery. ISBN 0-941483-59-2 9.95

THERE'S SOMETHING I'VE BEEN MEANING TO TELL YOU
Ed. by Loralee MacPike. 288 pp. Gay men and lesbians coming out
to their children. ISBN 0-941483-44-4 9.95

LIFTING BELLY by Gertrude Stein. Ed. by Rebecca Mark. 104 pp.
Erotic poetry. ISBN 0-941483-51-7 10.95

AFTER THE FIRE by Jane Rule. 256 pp. Warm, human novel by
this incomparable author. ISBN 0-941483-45-2 8.95

PLEASURES by Robbi Sommers. 204 pp. Unprecedented
eroticism. ISBN 0-941483-49-5 9.95

EDGEWISE by Camarin Grae. 372 pp. Spellbinding
adventure. ISBN 0-941483-19-3 9.95

FATAL REUNION by Claire McNab. 224 pp. 2nd Carol Ashton
Mystery. ISBN 0-941483-40-1 10.95

IN EVERY PORT by Karin Kallmaker. 228 pp. Jessica's sexy,
adventuresome travels. ISBN 0-941483-37-7 10.95

OF LOVE AND GLORY by Evelyn Kennedy. 192 pp. Exciting
WWII romance. ISBN 0-941483-32-0 10.95

CLICKING STONES by Nancy Tyler Glenn. 288 pp. Love
transcending time. ISBN 0-941483-31-2 9.95

SOUTH OF THE LINE by Catherine Ennis. 216 pp. Civil War
adventure.   ISBN 0-941483-29-0   8.95

WOMAN PLUS WOMAN by Dolores Klaich. 300 pp. Supurb
Lesbian overview.   ISBN 0-941483-28-2   9.95

THE FINER GRAIN by Denise Ohio. 216 pp. Brilliant young
college lesbian novel.   ISBN 0-941483-11-8   8.95

BEFORE STONEWALL: THE MAKING OF A GAY AND
LESBIAN COMMUNITY by Andrea Weiss & Greta Schiller.
96 pp., 25 illus.   ISBN 0-941483-20-7   7.95

OSTEN'S BAY by Zenobia N. Vole. 204 pp. Sizzling adventure
romance set on Bonaire.   ISBN 0-941483-15-0   8.95

LESSONS IN MURDER by Claire McNab. 216 pp. 1st Carol Ashton
Mystery.   ISBN 0-941483-14-2   10.95

YELLOWTHROAT by Penny Hayes. 240 pp. Margarita, bandit,
kidnaps Julia.   ISBN 0-941483-10-X   8.95

SAPPHISTRY: THE BOOK OF LESBIAN SEXUALITY by
Pat Califia. 3d edition, revised. 208 pp.   ISBN 0-941483-24-X   10.95

CHERISHED LOVE by Evelyn Kennedy. 192 pp. Erotic Lesbian
love story.   ISBN 0-941483-08-8   10.95

THE SECRET IN THE BIRD by Camarin Grae. 312 pp. Striking,
psychological suspense novel.   ISBN 0-941483-05-3   8.95

TO THE LIGHTNING by Catherine Ennis. 208 pp. Romantic
Lesbian 'Robinson Crusoe' adventure.   ISBN 0-941483-06-1   8.95

DREAMS AND SWORDS by Katherine V. Forrest. 192 pp.
Romantic, erotic, imaginative stories.   ISBN 0-941483-03-7   10.95

MEMORY BOARD by Jane Rule. 336 pp. Memorable novel
about an aging Lesbian couple.   ISBN 0-941483-02-9   12.95

THE ALWAYS ANONYMOUS BEAST by Lauren Wright Douglas.
224 pp. 1st Caitlin Reece Mystery.
                                            ISBN 0-941483-04-5   8.95

MURDER AT THE NIGHTWOOD BAR by Katherine V. Forrest.
240 pp. 2nd Kate Delafield Mystery.   ISBN 0-930044-92-4   11.95

WINGED DANCER by Camarin Grae. 228 pp. Erotic Lesbian
adventure story.   ISBN 0-930044-88-6   8.95

PAZ by Camarin Grae. 336 pp. Romantic Lesbian adventurer
with the power to change the world.   ISBN 0-930044-89-4   8.95

SOUL SNATCHER by Camarin Grae. 224 pp. A puzzle, an
adventure, a mystery — Lesbian romance.   ISBN 0-930044-90-8   8.95

THE LOVE OF GOOD WOMEN by Isabel Miller. 224 pp.
Long-awaited new novel by the author of the beloved *Patience
and Sarah*.   ISBN 0-930044-81-9   8.95

THE LONG TRAIL by Penny Hayes. 248 pp. Vivid adventures
of two women in love in the old west.   ISBN 0-930044-76-2   8.95

AN EMERGENCE OF GREEN by Katherine V. Forrest. 288
pp. Powerful novel of sexual discovery.   ISBN 0-930044-69-X   11.95

THE LESBIAN PERIODICALS INDEX edited by Claire Potter.
432 pp. Author & subject index.   ISBN 0-930044-74-6   12.95

DESERT OF THE HEART by Jane Rule. 224 pp. A classic;
basis for the movie *Desert Hearts*.   ISBN 0-930044-73-8   10.95

SEX VARIANT WOMEN IN LITERATURE by Jeannette
Howard Foster. 448 pp. Literary history.   ISBN 0-930044-65-7   8.95

A HOT-EYED MODERATE by Jane Rule. 252 pp. Hard-hitting
essays on gay life; writing; art.   ISBN 0-930044-57-6   7.95

AMATEUR CITY by Katherine V. Forrest. 224 pp. 1st Kate
Delafield Mystery.   ISBN 0-930044-55-X   10.95

THE SOPHIE HOROWITZ STORY by Sarah Schulman. 176 pp.
Engaging novel of madcap intrigue.   ISBN 0-930044-54-1   7.95

THE YOUNG IN ONE ANOTHER'S ARMS by Jane Rule.
224 pp. Classic Jane Rule.   ISBN 0-930044-53-3   9.95

AGAINST THE SEASON by Jane Rule. 224 pp. Luminous,
complex novel of interrelationships.   ISBN 0-930044-48-7   8.95

LOVERS IN THE PRESENT AFTERNOON by Kathleen Fleming.
288 pp. A novel about recovery and growth.   ISBN 0-930044-46-0   8.95

CONTRACT WITH THE WORLD by Jane Rule. 340 pp. Power-
ful, panoramic novel of gay life.   ISBN 0-930044-28-2   9.95

THIS IS NOT FOR YOU by Jane Rule. 284 pp. A letter to a
beloved is also an intricate novel.   ISBN 0-930044-25-8   8.95

OUTLANDER by Jane Rule. 207 pp. Short stories and essays by
one of our finest writers.   ISBN 0-930044-17-7   8.95

These are just a few of the many Naiad Press titles — we are the oldest and
largest lesbian/feminist publishing company in the world. We also offer an
enormous selection of lesbian video products. Please request a complete
catalog. We offer personal service; we encourage and welcome direct mail
orders from individuals who have limited access to bookstores carrying our
publications.

ODD GIRL OUT by Ann Bannon. ISBN 0-930044-83-5 5.95
I AM A WOMAN 84-3; WOMEN IN THE SHADOWS 85-1; each
JOURNEY TO A WOMAN 86-X; BEEBO BRINKER 87-8. Golden
oldies about life in Greenwich Village.

JOURNEY TO FULFILLMENT, A WORLD WITHOUT MEN, and 3.95
RETURN TO LESBOS. All by Valerie Taylor each

These are just a few of the many Naiad Press titles — we are the oldest and
largest lesbian/feminist publishing company in the world. Please request a
complete catalog. We offer personal service; we encourage and welcome
direct mail orders from individuals who have limited access to bookstores
carrying our publications.